Not Even A Moose

Not Even A Moose

By

Nancy Kay

Enjoy! Nancy Kay

Other Books By Nancy Kay

Sweet Deception
Wine And Spirits
Return To Intermezzo

Deadly Triad series

Book One: Deadly Reflection
Book Two: Deadly Revenge
Book Three: Deadly Encounter

Desert Breeze Publishing, Inc.
27305 W. Live Oak Rd #424
Castaic, CA 91384

http://www.DesertBreezePublishing.com

Copyright © 2017 by Nancy Kay
ISBN 13: 978-1-68294-873-6

Published in the United States of America
Publication Date: October 2017

Editor-In-Chief: Gail R. Delaney
Editor: Gail R. Delaney
Marketing Director: Jenifer Ranieri
Cover Artist: Carol Fiorillo

Cover Art Copyright by Desert Breeze Publishing, Inc © 2017

Dedication and Acknowledgment

Watertown, New York was the inspiration for writing *Not Even A Moose*. Situated not far from the eastern shore of Lake Ontario, Watertown often gets crippling lake effect snow in winter. I traveled to Watertown while researching the site for this book and was pleasantly surprised by the beauty and friendliness of this little town. I discovered The Apollo Restaurant, a Greek restaurant tucked away in a small plaza; a downtown square filled with charm; and Thompson Park, a beautiful multiuse setting just outside town. The Roswell P. Flower Memorial Library in downtown Watertown is magnificent. Built in 1903, the marble-faced two story building is a must see when visiting Watertown. Therefore, I dedicate my story to the town that gave me the inspiration to write Not Even A Moose.

Chapter One

December
Watertown, New York

Michael Donovan swiped at the tear that slid down his cheek. He was ten, darn it, almost eleven and he would not cry. Swallowing hard, Mike followed his dad into the vet's exam room.

Doc Gates held the door wide and when Mike hesitated, he laid a hand on his shoulder. "Put him on the table, Jim," he said to Mike's dad, and then squatted down, turning Mike to face him eye to eye. "I'm going to look your dog over, Mikey. From what your dad says he pulled a muscle, maybe dislocated his shoulder."

"He jumped off the porch. From the high end," Mike's voice hitched, and he bit down on his trembling lip.

Charley Gates stood. "Snoop is a strong, healthy dog. Why don't you come over by your dad, close to Snoop's head so he can see you? Not too close, just talk to him. Let him know you're there."

Mike sucked in a shaky breath and nodded. His knees trembled as he edged close to the big shiny table. His dad pulled him in front of him, placing a hand on each shoulder. The warmth of those strong, familiar hands steadied Mike.

His dad leaned down, his breath warm against Mike's ear. "Do like Doc said, son."

"Easy, Snoop. I'm here. Don't worry, fella, Doc Gates is the best. He'll fix you." His words sounded weak and funny, like he stood in a tunnel.

The wink Dr. Gates sent his way before turning to the trembling lab, along with his dad's firm grip, loosened knots in his belly. Tight, painful knots that had grabbed hold the moment he'd heard Snoop's sharp cry.

"I'm going to give Snoop something to ease his pain while I examine him, "explained Dr. Gates. "He'll look like he's sleeping. He'll be okay."

Mike just nodded, afraid his voice would squeak again if he tried to say anything. He sucked in a deep breath. Somehow Snoop always knew when he was upset, and he didn't want Snoop to be afraid or worry. He didn't know if dogs worried, but he wasn't taking that chance.

The doctor was right. Snoop's shoulder was dislocated, whatever that meant, but not broken. Assured by his dad, and the doctor, Mike decided their suggestion to wait in the other room was a good idea. Snoop had stopped crying out every time he moved. His dog was asleep, so there wasn't any reason for him to stay while Doc Gates fixed him.

Plus, his queasy stomach made the idea of waiting someplace else until it was all over a good idea.

But he couldn't sit still. He paced the waiting room and stopped at a window, peering through the cheerful, green wreath at snow drifting down. He'd bet there was already six inches on the ground, and the weather guy said there was more on the way.

He glanced around the long narrow waiting room. Chairs lined the walls and a small bench separated it into two sections. He'd been here many times, like for Snoop's regular check-ups, but never really paid much attention to things like the picture of a tabby cat on the wall at the far end of the room. Above Mike's head hung a picture of a happy chocolate lab, just like Snoop. "Neat," he said. Pictures worked better than signs and helped people sit in the right place. Cats with cats, dogs with dogs. "Neat," he repeated.

The office was connected to the Gates home by a covered walkway. As Mike turned from a window facing the house, the sound of a door slamming made his gaze snap back.

A slim figure appeared. She stomped down the shoveled walkway from the side door of the house. Mike figured it was a girl, because most girls had long hair and hers was pulled back into a long tail. She wasn't wearing a coat. Snow clung to her unprotected head like frosting on a dark cake as she stood, hands on hips, and glared at the door she'd slammed.

"Stupid girl," he muttered. "And she looks mad."

He figured she must be Dr. Gates' granddaughter, who he'd heard of from time to time, and knew he was older than her. Though from where he stood she looked almost as tall as him, and she looked steaming mad about something.

Her breath huffed out, a white cloud in the frosty air. Then she turned and headed down the walk away from the house. Mike frowned. Should he tell someone? It was freezing out there, and snowing. If she wandered too far she could be in trouble. His dad often warned him how dangerous the cold was if someone wasn't prepared, and that tall, skinny, angry looking girl sure as heck wasn't prepared.

When she rounded the corner of the house, disappearing from sight, he was about to knock on the exam room door when it swung open. His dad smiled and motioned him inside.

They went down a narrow hallway from the exam room to a small kennel. Inside an enclosure, Snoop lay very still. Dr. Gates stood by the opening adjusting a long tube attached to his dog's leg.

Mike sucked in a sharp breath and the doctor turned to face him. "He's fine, Mikey. He'll be out a bit longer, but he'll feel much better when he wakes up."

"What's that?" Mike stepped closer and pointed to the tubing that

2

was held in place by thick white tape. His gaze slid from the bandaged leg to a bag holding what looked like water attached to a hook inside the kennel.

"It's some... ah, medicine to help Snoop heal faster. I fixed his shoulder, but he'll be sore for a few days. Maybe he'll limp a bit, too, but with some rest and care he'll be like new before Christmas."

Christmas was two weeks away, which seemed way too long for Mike. "Can I touch him?"

"Sure, he's still out, but I believe he'll know you're here if you touch him. Talk to him." He smiled as Mike inched forward and gently stroked Snoop's head. "That's it. Love, it's the best medicine going."

Assured as Snoop's chest steadily rose and fell, Mike glanced up and smiled at the doctor as he stroked the warm fur. Then he remembered. "Oh, Doctor Gates, I think your granddaughter might be in danger."

Charley Gates straightened. "Oh, how so?"

Mike relayed what he'd seen and the doctor's stiff shoulders relaxed.

"Something wrong, Charley?" Mike's dad asked, stepping forward.

The doctor gestured for his dad to step away from the kennel. "Thanks for letting me know, Mike. I'll check on Samantha, you keep your eye on Snoop for me."

Mike nodded and eased his hip onto the lip of the kennel. He continued to stroke Snoop's soft ears, but *his* ears were tuned in to the quiet conversation between his dad and the doctor a few feet away. He'd been warned about listening to what wasn't meant for him, but the two men were only a couple feet away. If they didn't want him to hear them they'd have moved on down the hall. So, if he overheard them it wasn't his fault.

"Our granddaughter Samantha isn't happy with her parents. To be honest, Jim, Ellen and I aren't too happy either. Samantha is only six, and for the first five years of her life they came from out east and spent the holidays with us."

Jim grinned. "I still can't believe my childhood pal is a surgeon in a big city hospital. I'd always hoped our kids would grow up together like Charley and I."

"So did I, Jim, so did I. Chuck inherited the doctor gene, only he opted to treat two legged patients. I'm not disappointed. He's good at what he does, and he's happy. That's what matters. Melissa, Sam's mom, is a beautiful, talented woman. Unfortunately, Watertown, New York doesn't offer much opportunity for a specialized surgeon like Chuck or a high class interior decorator like Melissa. So Boston is their home."

"I take it Samantha's not happy about spending Christmas in Boston," said Jim.

3

"She's not. Sam inherited my love for animals and I've looked forward to watching her grow and seeing where she's headed in life. Spending time with her at Christmas gave me that opportunity."

"Hmmm, I take it Sam's parents aren't too pleased by her early career choice. Christ, Charley, she can't be more than six. Why get so bent over a six year old's dream?"

"They think it's a phase she'll grow out of it if she's exposed to another lifestyle. One *they'd* prefer for her. I know better. I'm living proof that once the bug bites you, it sticks. I knew the minute I nursed a sick squirrel under the guidance of old Doc. Matthews what I wanted to be. I was six at the time, same as Sam." Charley shook his head. "I worry about her, Jim."

"Surely they'll let her spend time with you and Ellen."

"Oh yeah, they will. I'm going to make a deal with them. A selfish one, but nonetheless, I think it'll work." He paused and stepped over to check on Mike and Snoop. "How's it going?"

Without looking up, Mike ran a finger along Snoop's whiskered muzzle. "His eyes fluttered once, and he gave a big sigh, like when he's all sleepy and comfy."

"Good, that's good. You keep doing what you're doing and he'll be coming around real soon."

Mike nodded, never taking his eyes off Snoop. He didn't want to let on that he'd been listening to them. Although in his opinion, Samantha was getting a raw deal. No wonder she was mad.

"Anyhow, Jim," continued the doctor moments later, "Christmas has always been a special time for us, a time to get away and have a quiet holiday in private. You've seen our camp, haven't you?"

"I wouldn't call it a camp, more like a second home. I loved going there with Chuck over the years. You always went there for Christmas and then came back to town for New Year's."

"We did. Still do. It's a tradition we started when Chuck was just a boy and when he married Melissa and Samantha came along for five years we continued that tradition. Then this year, all of a sudden things changed."

Mike glanced over his shoulder. The sadness in the doctor's voice surprised him, and the way the older man rubbed at the frown lines between his eyes tugged at his heart. He waited, hoping his dad would say something to make Dr. Gates feel better. His dad was good at making you feel better when something bad happened.

"I'm going to suggest that as long as I'm able Samantha will spend Christmas at the cabin with Ellen and me."

"Whoa, Charley, that's some deal. Think they'll go for it?"

Charley slipped his hand into his pockets. "For a surgeon and his socially active wife the holiday season is a whirlwind of obligations and parties. I'm assuming a six year old underfoot is a problem, especially a

4

stubborn six year old female who digs in her heels and rejects even the nicest, most entertaining babysitters." He grinned. "She got the family tradition gene, along with a tad of her Grandpa's stubbornness. Wish me luck."

*****

Samantha Gates huddled beneath the branches of a tall evergreen. She drew her knees tight against her chest, rested her forehead on them, and sobbed.

They wouldn't let her. No matter what Grandpa did, her parents were going to drag her back to Boston and stick her with that stupid babysitter.

On Christmas.

Oh, they'd be there to do Christmas morning, after she'd spent Christmas Eve alone. Alone except for the stupid sitter who'd keep trying to read *'Twas the Night Before Christmas* to cheer her up. She'd fake it, and be polite because, after all, it was Christmas Eve and dear old Mrs. Olson would worry if she seemed unhappy. Then, if the sitter told her parents, her butt would be in a sling.

That's what Grandpa called it when you were in trouble.

She lifted her head and wiped her damp cheeks, forcing a shaky smile. Nobody read her favorite Christmas story like Grandpa.

Nobody.

Before he got the emergency call, he'd winked and told her to go out and play in the snow while he talked to her parents. She didn't feel much like playing, and she didn't believe talking to her mom and dad would change anything. When she'd asked her mom what they were going to talk about, she'd been told not to get her hopes up and to quit being so stubborn.

That's when she'd slammed out the door, ignoring her mom's order to stop.

Once outside she'd crawled under the branches of her favorite pine tree where the ground was covered with needles. A perfect hide out to have a good cry and watch the snow fall.

Now she shivered and her fingers hurt. She was about to give in and return to the house when footsteps crunching on the new snow caught her attention. She leaned down, peering out, hoping it was Grandpa bringing good news. Her heart sank and tears filled her eyes when she realized it was just the kid with the hurt dog.

She inched closer to the tree trunk and hugged her knees tighter.

The boots stepped closer, and Sam covered her mouth to keep him from hearing the ragged sobs she couldn't seem to stop. The boot clad feet stopped, turned in a circle, and then the boy dropped to his knees and pushed aside thick branches hiding her.

"Hey, you all right?"

Sam covered her face with both hands. "Go away."

Instead of listening, he ducked down and crawled in beside her. "Why are you crying? Are you hurt? I saw you earlier and you looked mad. Now you're sad. What's the deal?"

"I'm not crying, stupid."

"Yeah, you are." He settled on his butt right in front of her. "It's no big deal if you have a good reason to cry, but you're the stupid one out in this weather without a coat. Look at me, will ya?"

She sniffed, hard, and lowered her hands. His frown softened, and he smiled, revealing a crooked tooth and his eyes, a funny greenish gold in the dim light, were rimmed in telltale red.

Sam wiped her nose with the back of her hand. She frowned and sniffed again. "Have you been crying, too?"

His smile faded and he kind of jerked back. Then he sighed and rested his elbows on his crossed knees. "Maybe a little. My dog got hurt, and I was scared."

Forgetting her troubles for the moment, Sam reached out and touched him. "Oh, my grandpa can fix him. I'm sure," she added, and got onto her knees, ready to crawl out and get help for her sad new friend.

His smiled reappeared, and his funny, crooked toothed grin made her tummy jitter. Despite the cold, warmth spread through her as she returned his smile.

"Doc Gates is your grandpa."

Sam nodded. "Yes, he's my grandpa, and my name is Samantha. Samantha Gates."

"Hi, Samantha. My name is Mike Donovan." His grin widened. "Not Stupid. Come on, I want to check on my dog, and you need to get warm."

Chapter Two

Twenty Years Later...

Mike Donovan pulled his truck to the berm, slid it into park, and unsnapped his seatbelt. "What the hell?"

A large boxy trailer lay at an angle, half off the road, half on. It was hitched to a hefty pickup and its rear door gaped open, hanging by a single hinge. The hitch itself was twisted like a damn pretzel.

On the ground near the lopsided trailer, glistening red in the glow of his trucks headlights, was a trail of streaks and splotches. Mike frowned, and his gaze shifted to several men gathered around the wreckage, gray shadows in the fast fading light.

Snowflakes drifted on the air, stirred by a light breeze. He wasn't fooled. In the blink of an eye innocent flakes often turned deadly, driven by relentless, pounding wind.

He pulled on a knit cap, snapped tight the collar of his uniform jacket and exited the truck. Cold air bit with sharp teeth. He hunched deep into down layers and tugged on thick gloves.

"Hey, Donovan." One of the men near the upturned trailer separated from the others and made his way toward Mike.

"Al, what the hell's going on here?"

Fellow Federal Wildlife officer Alan Murray approached, sidestepping bits and pieces of wreckage and skirting the dark splotches. Snow sprinkled his dark hair. Longtime friends, both on and off the job, Al wore the same uniform. He also happened to be married to Mike's big sister Jane.

He jerked his head toward the wreck. "A frickin' mess, Mike, that's what's going on." He stopped, pulled his cell phone from an inside pocket and checked the screen. "Timing couldn't be worse," he muttered, shoving the phone away.

Standing shoulder to shoulder, surveying the damage, Mike asked, "Hasn't my big sis made you a daddy yet?"

"Would I be out here dealing with this mess if she had?" Al shivered, cast a disparaging eye skyward and turned up his collar. "I'm actually off duty and was on my way home. With Jane due any day, I'm on leave until after New Year's. If our little guy doesn't make his debut by then the doc says he'll help things along. We're hoping it doesn't come to that."

"Waiting must be tough. But what's the deal here?" Mike glanced

7

around. "Where's the body?"

"No body, just one banged up, pissed off moose."

Mike stared at his friend. "Did you say moose?"

"I did." Al turned and laughed. "The look on your face. Priceless. And buddy, I'm afraid it's *your* moose now." He brushed snow from his hair and scrutinized the surrounding forest. "You're the one who talked me into becoming a Federal Wildlife Officer, remember?"

Mike scowled at his friend. "Don't remind me."

"'You'll love it, Al,' you told me. We get to carry guns and animals don't shoot back.'"

Grinning now, Mike eased his hands into his pockets. "What did I know? We already had degrees in criminal justice, both loved being around animals." He shrugged. "We made it through training. No walk in the park," he added.

Al gave Mike's arm a good-natured poke. "Yeah, and both ended up back in the snow capital of New York freezing our butts off protecting those critters we love so much."

"Not a bad gig for two geeky losers."

"I'll say," Al replied. "I got razzed for being a geek and you for having red hair, a cockeyed tooth, *and* being a geek."

Mike tapped the corner of his mouth, and smiled. "Women love my snaggletooth look, and can't wait to get their hands in my 'strawberry blond' -- their descriptions not mine -- locks. We survived," he added, "'Cause we're smart, and we stuck together."

A sudden gust of wind rattled the trailer's damaged door, threatening to rip it from the remaining hinge.

"The wind's picking up. Snow, too. Fill me in on this ah... moose situation, and then get the hell home to your pregnant wife."

*****

The woman behind the counter in Brown's General Supply and Grocery glanced up at the musical tinkling of the bell over the door. Her gray hair was arranged in short layers, and hazel eyes, set wide on a youthful face, crinkled around the edges when she smiled. "Samantha Ellen Gates."

Sam stopped, pulling the door shut behind her. The tinkling bell overhead stilled. She broke into a smile, closed the distance between them and reached out to grasp Lillian Brown's extended hands. "Mrs. Brown, you haven't changed a bit."

Lillian gave Sam a gentle pat on the cheek. "A polite lie," she responded, chuckling. "But you have, my dear." She ran light fingers over Sam's hair. "You've done something fun to your hair, and you still have gorgeous blue eyes. Plus, you've filled out very nicely, Samantha."

Sam's cheeks flushed as the older woman's gaze skimmed over her.

Lil squeezed her hand, winked and gestured for Sam to come around behind the counter. "I'll admit I had my doubts at times. You were skinny as a rail and had wild unruly hair. Gypsy locks I think your mother called it."

Sam winced, remembering. Her mother's discontent with her ugly duck daughter had been no secret, but Lillian Brown had always said just the opposite. "Even back then you called me beautiful. I've never forgotten that," said Sam, sighing long and hard when Lillian's arms closed around her.

"Truth's the truth, young lady, and though I liked your mother and respected her, in my opinion she needed to stop fussing and see what was inside her daughter and not harp so much about the outside. Time took care of her concerns, though, and she should be satisfied that despite all the criticism she heaped on you things turned around."

Sam gave Lil a quick squeeze and stepped back, loosening the scarf she'd wrapped around her neck to fight off the cold. Brown's was toasty warm inside. "I'm afraid I'm still a disappointment in some respects."

"And why would that be?"

"I've switched direction, much to Mother's dismay. I took all pre-med in college, like she wanted, but then things changed."

"What things, honey." Lil urged, crossing her arms.

"My interest shifted, or maybe I should say focused, and it turns out my skills to heal and treat lean more toward four-legged patients."

Lil's smile stretched ear to ear. "You're going to be a vet like your grandpa. Bless you child, and bless whatever turned you around and set you straight. Here, have a Peppermint Patti."

Laughing, Sam dug into the huge glass jar on the counter, unwrapped one and popped the chocolate-coated mint into her mouth.

She'd had doubts about her decision given her mom's outrage and prediction she'd regret her choice, but her excellent grades opened doors. "I've been accepted into one of the top veterinary schools in the country, and spent last summer doing an internship at an animal rehabilitation facility in Canada."

"Good for you. How was it, the internship?"

"I learned *so* much, plus, it took me a couple thousand miles away from Mother's disdain for the whole summer."

Lillian chuckled, and Sam took a deep breath, gazing around the room. Neat rows with shelves contained everything from Band Aids to canned goods, and a floor to ceiling cooler took up one whole wall. The store's rough log walls created a warm, woodsy feel, and flames danced over logs in a raised fireplace tucked in the far corner.

"You're right," Sam admitted. "I've changed. Yet stepping through your door was like stepping back in time. Here in Watertown, in this store, I was never judged. It was while spending time here with my grandparents that I discovered what I wanted to be. Needed to be," she corrected, and turned her head when the bell over the door chimed.

A blast of frigid air accompanied the man who entered. "Hey, Lil," he stomped snow from thick soled boots. "Wind's picking up. Maybe you'd better think about closing up early." He pulled off his knit cap, gave Sam a nod and a polite hello.

"Danny, you remember Samantha Gates. She's here to spend the holidays with her grandparents."

Dan Stone did a double take. "Sam? You're Sam Gates, Charley and Ellen's granddaughter?"

Lil exchanged a smug 'told you so' look with Sam.

"That's me, Skinny Sam."

Dan did a blatant head to toe perusal. "You sure did turn around, Sam. Maybe I should call you Samantha, now, huh?" He rubbed the side of his face, grinning. "Sorry about the Skinny Sam reference, but hell, you were a damn scarecrow back in the day."

"What can I get you, Danny?" asked Lil.

"Do you have any more of those little white lights? You know, the ones that flash on and off? Ginny says our tree looks naked. Needs more flash and glitter, she says."

"They're on the back shelf near the boxed icicles."

As Danny went for his lights, Lil turned to Sam. "Where are you headed, honey? It looks like the weather is turning."

"I'm heading to Grandpa's camp. It's been too many years since we've had Christmas there together, and with me heading off to vet school soon it may be our last chance for a while."

"Aren't they going with you? That's a long stretch of backwoods road to travel alone, especially on a night like this."

"I spoke with them on my cell phone just before I got here. They'd planned to follow me up, but Grandma said Grandpa had a touch of indigestion and wanted to wait until tomorrow. She wanted me to come there, but their place is a couple miles the other way and I'd already come this far. I'd rather keep going."

Danny Stone placed two boxes of white mini lights on the counter and overheard their exchange. "Sam, that road to Charley's camp can close up real fast."

"I have an SUV, Danny, and I've not forgotten how to drive around here. I spent many a holiday plowing through drifts to reach that camp."

Danny frowned, shaking his head. "You mentioned a cell phone. That's smart, but sometimes the signal is touchy around here, especially where you're heading. Just be careful and take your time. Having a good supply of firewood wouldn't hurt. These storms can shut down the power in the blink of an eye."

Sam picked up one of the baskets stacked by the counter. "I'm prepared. I just need to grab a few things. If it makes you feel any better, a few winter's ago Grandpa installed a generator at camp."

"He's a smart man, always was," said Danny, "but you gotta get there in one piece first."

Lil rang up Dan's lights and handed him change. "I'll be closing at noon on Christmas Eve, and we'll be closed all day on Christmas. The day after, too," she added. "My Herb says everyone should stay in and stretch out the holiday. We'll be staying in and stretching it out. That way we'll be ready for the rush before the New Year's celebrations."

"Sounds like a good plan, Lil. A Merry Christmas to you and Herb. Same to you and yours, Sam, and safe travels," he added. Clutching his purchase, Dan stepped into the wind, pulling the door shut behind him.

Arms crossed, Lil rubbed her hands up and down them, chasing the sudden chill as she studied the snow pelting the store's front window. "Are you sure you shouldn't head to Charley and Ellen's, Samantha?"

Sam wrapped one arm around Lil's rigid shoulder and gave a little squeeze. "I've dealt with lake effect snow many times. This storm will more than likely peak overnight, and by tomorrow the wind will shift. I'd rather be at the cabin all toasty warm with a path cleared to the door when Grandma and Grandpa arrive. The cabin is less than an hour from here, and the storm's just getting started. I can make it."

Lillian glanced at the time. "Then you'd better get moving. You told your grandparents your plans?"

"Yes, when I talked to them just before I came into the store. Grandma said to be careful and that they'd see me early tomorrow."

"Hmm, I'd feel better if you'd wait out the storm." Lil wrung up Sam's purchases. She tossed a handful of Peppermint Patties into the bag. "On the house," she said, and walked with Sam to the door.

Sam pointed to her Honda Pilot parked in front of the store. "That big guy will get me there without any trouble." She hugged Lil, and flipped up her hood. "Merry Christmas, and give my best to Mr. Brown. I'll stop in after the holidays before I head back."

Fighting the wind, Sam pulled out her cell and tried to contact her grandparents to check on her grandfather. Grandpa was in good shape, but still... Frowning at the lack of signal, Sam tossed her new supplies into the back seat, grabbed her snowbrush and cleared the windows before sliding behind the wheel. She hesitated. The relentless snow encompassed the vehicle like thick, white fog. Should she head back to her grandparents?

Thoughts of that cozy cabin in the woods, a crackling fire and several recently purchased bottles of her favorite wine helped her decide. With XM radio turned low, Sam set out, humming along with holiday tunes. Once she reached higher ground and got a signal she'd call her grandparents and assure them she'd reached the cabin safe and sound.

Chapter Three

"You're telling me a moose," Mike held wide spread hands by his ears, "as in big antlers and butt ugly face, escaped when the truck wrecked?"

"That's right, a six to seven month old moose. Only this one doesn't have antlers yet. It was being transported to Adirondack Rehab. That's all I know." Al checked his phone again. "I feel like crap dumping this on you. Damn it, you're off duty and--"

"I can manage. I'll put in for OT and give myself a nice Christmas bonus. Hell, how far can an injured moose go? Judging by the amount of blood I'm seeing, his luck may have run out by now and I'll end up dealing with a moose corpse. I'll check in with headquarters and see what they want me to do."

Al nodded. "I just spoke to them and they said it wasn't worth risking men and equipment if the weather gets worse. I feel bad for the damn moose, though."

Mike chuckled. "A statement I never thought I'd hear. Go on home to Jane. I was on my way to Brown's Supply to pick up a couple things for my mom. It'll only take a few minutes. Then I'll follow up with headquarters and try my hand at moose tracking."

"Sounds good. Take care, Mike. Happy moose hunting and if I don't see you before, Merry Christmas."

As Al trudged through falling snow to his truck, Mike moved closer to the accident scene. The blood trail and hoof prints led into the woods. He knelt for a closer look, then stood and gazed into a wall of bare-branched trees.

He checked with his superior, and his instructions were to monitor the weather and act accordingly. "Whatever the hell that means," muttered Mike. He made a mental note of the accident site, the direction the tracks led, and headed toward Lil and Herb Brown's store.

Just outside town a large SUV approached heading the direction from which he'd come. The vehicle's headlights barely cut through the wall of white and, keeping his eyes on the road, he muttered as they passed, "What idiot is out on a night like this?"

The town square appeared through the white haze. Colorful lights strung between poles lining the square cast a cheerful, hazy glow as he passed beneath them. Windows were ablaze with tiny white lights, and a few brave souls Mike pegged as last minute shoppers hustled along the sidewalk.

"Better get your butts home, folks," he said, and eased to the curb in front of Brown's Supply. Through the fast falling flakes he made out Lil inside the store chatting as she checked someone out.

True to holiday tradition, the windows flanking the door were a winter wonderland. One side displayed rolling hills made of cotton and tiny houses strung along make-believe streets. Herb Brown's American Flyer train circled the miniature village, disappearing through a tunnel and emerging on the opposite side. The train's tiny headlight lit the way, and the engine's smokestack trailed artificial smoke. The train was vintage 40's or 50's, and Mike couldn't remember a Christmas when it didn't circle through that make-believe village.

The opposite window held a nativity, another tradition. A trio of camels led the way to the handmade manger leaving footprints behind in a swirl of real sand. Herb insisted on depicting it this way, claiming there was no snow in Bethlehem that night.

Lil glanced up when he entered. "Mike Donovan, what brings you out on a night like this?"

"Duty calls, Lillian, and I never miss a chance to see the most gorgeous girl in Watertown."

If he wasn't mistaken, Lil Brown blushed as she handed change to her customer. "Hurry home, honey," she called after to the young boy, who brushed past Mike and let in a blast of cold air on his way out.

"I'm about to cash out, Mike. What can I get you?"

Mike detoured to the large cooler. "Mom forgot whipped cream for her pies. I was on my way home and she called while I was checking out an accident northwest of town."

"Anybody hurt?"

"Nobody you know. Apparently the only injury is a moose."

Lil's eyes widened. "A moose? Why, we haven't had a moose around here in years." She frowned, tugging her left ear. "Unless you count the one a couple years ago that hung out near the school until your co-workers came around and hauled him away."

"Yeah, no kidding? I must have been in training when that happened. No, I'm told this poor guy was orphaned this spring and after outgrowing facilities somewhere west of here was being transported to the Adirondack center. The truck slid off the road, broke open, and the moose got away."

"How big is this runaway moose?"

"He's about six or seven months, so I'd say about pony or small horse size, and he's injured."

Lil began gathering the day's sales slips. "That's too bad. This miserable storm could be the end for an injured animal. Especially since folks north of here have heard what they claim was a wolf recently."

Mike set two containers of whipped cream on the counter. He'd heard the same, and until Lil reminded him had forgotten about the

13

report. Something else to consider, he pondered, and turned to stare out at the driving snow.

"Has your sister made you an uncle yet?"

Mike grinned and reached for his wallet. "Not yet. I think the waiting is driving Al crazy, though."

"Whipped cream's on the house."

"What? No, Lil, I can't do that."

"Call it an early present. I'm done figuring my sales for today and checking you out will just screw me up tomorrow." She studied him as she bagged up the two canisters. "You're worried about that moose, aren't you?"

"I'd forgotten about that wolf report. It wasn't verified, but like occasional moose sightings, wolves do make their way into our area once in a while." He shrugged. "I'd hate to see all the work folks put into saving a baby moose go to waste."

"You said it was injured. How bad?"

"Al didn't know for sure, but there was plenty of blood around that smashed up trailer. This snow isn't going to make it easy to track. I may just have to wait until the storm breaks."

The phone on the counter shrilled.

Lil snatched up the receiver. "That's probably Herb telling me to close up and get the heck home."

Mike froze while pulling on his gloves when the color left Lil's cheeks, and her dark eyes focused on him. "Mike Donovan is with me right now. He's heading that direction. I'll tell him to watch for her."

"What is it, Lil?" Mike skirted the counter. He took Lil's arm and made her sit on a nearby stool.

"Herb says they've rushed Charley Gates to the hospital." Lil pushed at her hair with a shaky hand. "Poor Ellen must be frantic."

"Does she need help? I can--"

"No, Ellen's with Charley, it's Samantha they're worried about. She's on her way to the cabin and they can't reach her."

"Sam Gates is *here*?"

"Yes, she stopped in a short time ago on the way to her grandparents' cabin."

"Shit. The girl always was stubborn and headstrong. Why would she head up there by herself in a snowstorm, especially when her grandpa was sick?"

Lil narrowed her eyes at Mike. "She's not stubborn, just confident. And, she doesn't know about the hospital. Her grandmother told her Charley had indigestion and they'd join Sam at the cabin tomorrow."

"So Sam just took off by herself? Damn it. What is she driving?"

"A big SUV. She's got a cell phone, but Herb said Ellen was unable to reach her."

Mike rubbed his neck, his gaze drawn to the front window. "In this

14

weather it's no surprise. The reception around here is crappy on good days." He rested a hand on Lil's shoulder. "Can you make it home?"

Lil patted his hand and shoved to her feet. "Yes, I'm fine. The call just took me by surprise. Charley and Ellen are like family."

Mike pulled on his gloves and dug out his keys. "I'll head back to the accident scene to see if I can pick up a trail. My parents' place is out that way. I figured if need be I could hunker down there until the storm lets up, but this changes things."

Mike waited while Lil locked the store and walked her to her truck. He cleaned off the windows while she warmed up the engine, stepping up when she rolled down the window. "It looks like the plow has been through. Take your time and you'll be all right."

"It's less than two miles, Mike. I can drive it with my eyes closed."

He grinned, blinking away snow clinging to his eyelashes. "Keep them open, okay."

She covered the hand he'd placed on the doorframe. "Be careful. The road to the Gates cabin won't be plowed."

"How did you know that's where I'm going?"

"I know you, honey. You were fretting about a helpless moose, now you've got another worry. Samantha Gates may be a bit headstrong, but she's pretty self-sufficient."

Mike pointed a finger at her. "Straight home, lady, and maybe I'll get lucky and rescue a headstrong female *and* a banged up moose."

The snow swallowed up Lil's taillights less than a block down the street. As Mike began to clear his windows and lights something crunched beneath his foot. He bent down, searched around and shook his head when he discovered a cell phone buried in the snow. "Shit, I'll bet this is Samantha's. No wonder they couldn't reach her."

The screen was smashed. He tried to open it, but the Galaxy S6 was password protected. "Hmm, maybe the girl isn't so clueless anymore," he muttered. Then the screen went black.

He tossed the dead phone into his truck and finished clearing his windows and lights. The snow just kept coming as he swung around and headed west on Arsenal Street, crossing over the four lane, Route 81, on his way back to the accident scene.

Mike eyed the bagged Reddi Whip beside him. "Sorry, Mom. I'm off on a wild moose chase, or saving a stubborn young lady's butt. Take your pick."

*****

Once the cheerful holiday lights faded in her rearview mirror, Samantha focused on the road ahead. The surrounding forest broke the wind, keeping drifts to a minimum. Her Pilot held steady as she forged

15

new tracks on the lonely stretch of road. The only sign of another person out and about was the truck heading into town she'd passed earlier. As she got closer to her turnoff, she also passed a deserted trailer in a ditch. She slowed, but the trailer was covered with snow and there wasn't a soul around so she pushed on.

The dash lights cast an eerie glow, and the SUV's headlights barely lit the road more than a few feet ahead. Sam's firm grip on the wheel and steady gaze into the undulating wall of snow never faltered. She turned right just east of Sackets Harbor, a virtual ghost town this time of year, and headed northwest.

A tall evergreen's dark outline appeared on the left. "Okay, okay," she muttered, straining her eyes against the wall of white. "I remember that tree, and the turnoff is less than a mile."

Slowing to a crawl, wipers clicking, defroster humming, Sam straightened and leaned forward. Up ahead on the left a break in the tree line came into view. "Aha, there's Gate's Lane." She sucked in a deep breath, slowed and turned. A barely discernable pathway wound through the trees. The Pilot's tires dug in and the vehicle bumped off the road onto the narrow lane. She blew out a relieved breath as the relentless snow eased under protection of tall trees lining the way. The forest closed in around her, and she gaged close to a foot of snow coated the narrow pathway. Her Pilot moved forward at a slow, steady pace.

Tense muscles relaxed, and as Bing crooned about dreams of a white Christmas, her mind wandered and she recalled Lillian Brown's words. She *had* outgrown her gawkiness, and Lillian had noticed. The woman was salt of the earth. She didn't say what she didn't mean.

As Sam matured, some of those physical changes had put a smile on her mother's perfectly made up face. Her mother bragged when Sam chose pre-med and shot to the head of her class.

But when Sam changed course, Mom's smile faded and bragging became nagging.

For the first time in her life, though, Sam had followed her heart, and the satisfaction, the joy, derived from doing so was immense.

Visits with her grandparents bolstered her self-confidence and helped her pursue something she'd longed for all of her life.

Each visit took her away from the constant upheaval and ongoing emotional tug of war with her mother. She loved the woman. Melissa Monroe Gates made sure her daughter never wanted for anything money could buy, unaware all Sam ever wanted was her mother's trust and support.

Sam sensed, rather than saw, the beginning of a slight rise in the road. She switched mental gears and pictured what lay ahead. Once the forest around her thinned, the Pilot began to climb.

Wind slammed the vehicle when it broke from the sheltering trees. Navigating a sharp right turn, Sam's grip tightened on the wheel. She kept her speed steady as they climbed. "Come on, come on, I've made it this far."

With a bump and slide, she crested the hill. Snow billowed as the Pilot plowed through much deeper snow and huge drifts. The clearing below where the cabin stood was shrouded in wind driven snow. Sam's heart pounded as she pressed on, finding her way more from memory than sight.

The nose of the SUV dipped and plowed through feet of snow now instead of inches. Then just as the faint outline of the cabin emerged, the steering wheel suddenly jerked. Sam fought for control. Innocent looking drifts grabbed like steel hands and the Pilot lurched sideways on the narrow path, then back, jolting to a stop. Her seatbelt tightened. Despite layers of winter clothes, the sudden stop shot pain through her body.

Her breath came in short gasps. Dazed, Sam squeezed her eyes shut, fighting panic. Sleazy nausea rose in her throat, and dizziness came in waves. Several minutes passed before she settled enough to open her eyes and cut the engine. Except for the howling wind, silence closed in around her. No whirring heater, no wipers' mad, slapping sweep.

The Pilot's headlights pierced the swirling white void, and Sam squeaked out a startled gasp when two, ghostly green eyes suddenly appeared in the twin beams.

Chapter Four

"Holy cow, a damn deer." Sam pressed her palm to her pounding heart. "Scared the crap out of me," she murmured, scowling through the windshield at the eerie reflections.

She released her seatbelt and took a deep breath. Everything had shifted. Her backpack had slid onto the floor. Wrapped packages in the back were a jumbled mess, and God knew how her carefully packed wine stash had fared.

"Unless I can back out of this snowbank I'll have to carry all this crap to the cabin on foot. Wonderful."

The Pilot had slid sideways into a ditch. With the tilted angle and the way land sloped toward the clearing below, its headlights lit the narrow lane. The animal with spooky eyes hadn't moved.

Sam leaned forward and peered through the frosty windshield. At first she feared she'd hit the poor thing, but the shadowy outline didn't appear close enough. She fought the door open and slid out, sinking knee deep in snow.

After a fast assessment of her situation, it was clear her trusty SUV had met its match. She waded around to the rear and opened the hatch. Gathering an emergency light -- *thank you, Grandpa* -- and a duffle with the bare essentials, she plowed her way to the passenger door and collected her backpack. Her ribs protested when she slid her arms through the straps and settled the pack on her back. The pack contained sweats for sleeping, an extra pair of leggings, a sweater, and, of course, her Christmas Eve outfit. She'd crammed a lot into that backpack, but thank goodness nothing too heavy.

She reached across, turned off the lights, and got her keys. Not that the vehicle was going anywhere if by chance someone happened along, but the keychain also held keys to the cabin and the attached garage/barn. If she was lucky she'd be able to reach the structures without getting buried in snow.

Head bent against driving wind and snow, Sam left the Pilot behind, headed down hill, and jerked to a stop at the sound of a muffled grunt. Her eyes opened wide. "Oh, my God. You're not a deer," she said, standing eye-to-eye not four feet from a moose.

The animal grunted again, and the whites of its eyes flashed as it tried to move away.

Sam's gaze ran over the gangly, long legged animal. A deep gash ran from the moose's shoulder half way down its front leg. Dried blood, or maybe frozen blood, covered his chocolate brown coat, and when it tried to move the injured leg buckled.

The moose went down, folding onto the snow and leaving a smear of fresh blood on the pristine white. Dropping her duffle, Sam knelt beside the helpless beast. "Easy, there big fella," she spoke softly and quietly. Her heart twisted when the young moose let out an almost human sounding moan.

She had no idea where the moose had come from. Considering its size and her experience at the retreat in Canada, she guessed it to be about seven months old. It was a bull, judging by his dark face and two bumps on its head. The bumps would become antlers, but not until after the first year. She gently ran a hand over its large nose. It moaned softly, but didn't panic.

"You're used to people, aren't you, fella?" He turned his head at her touch and gazed at her with dark, liquid eyes.

Blood streamed from the shoulder gash, dripping into the snow. No way could she assess and treat the injured moose in the middle of a snowstorm. The dim outline of the cabin and garage came and went with the shifting wind. Sam figured they needed to cover at least fifty feet to reach shelter. "Okay, Bullwinkle," she murmured, unwinding the scarf from around her neck. "I'm sure you won't like this, and it will probably hurt like heck, but it's the best I've got. If I can get you out of this storm, maybe, just maybe I can keep you from bleeding to death."

She wrapped the scarf around the moose's neck and worked her way around behind the prone animal. After several tries, she managed to help him to a sitting position. The injured leg hung limp and useless now, and his soft moans broke her heart.

At last, as if sensing the need, the moose heaved his body and with Sam lifting with the scarf rose on three shaky legs.

"Okay, okay." Sam shouldered the discarded duffle and wedged the flashlight under one arm. "Let's see if we can make it, fella."

*****

"Damn." He'd almost missed the turnoff. Cursing, Mike eased to a stop on the snow-covered road and shifted into reverse. Faint tire tracks were visible weaving between the trees past a sign on sturdy log supports encrusted with snow that read Gates Lane. He pulled out his cell phone. Better let someone know where he was heading.

No signal.

"Bullheaded female," grumbled Mike, and tossed the phone onto the console between the seats. He eased his truck off the road and lined up with the fading tread marks that he assumed belonged to Sam's SUV. At least there was a path, a damn trail to follow.

Unlike the disappearing moose.

About a mile back when he'd reached the accident scene the truck was gone, but the smashed trailer still lay in the ditch. Any sign of the injured moose had disappeared under fresh fallen snow. He remembered where the tracks had entered the woods, but the trail stopped there. He'd slipped out of his warm truck and faced the driving snow to check, to make sure the injured beast wasn't lying in the woods close by. No luck there, so he'd pushed on.

His mood darkened now, as he thought of the poor animal suffering somewhere in the cold, white madness or worse yet, dying a horrible death if the scent of fresh blood drew in predators.

Damn it, he should turn the hell around and head home before the roads were impassable. If that crazy girl made it this far, she should be able to get to the cabin. The idea of reaching the remote cabin and being forced to wait out the storm with her did not improve his mood.

Three days before Christmas and this storm threatened to shut down his escape route back to civilization. "Shit!" He bounced over a fallen branch. "If I had a choice, I'd rather hole up with the damn moose."

He kept moving, and as he lurched along the unplowed lane, a memory of one long ago winter day flashed in his mind's eye.

Without coat or hat, Sam Gates had run out into a snowstorm because she didn't get her friggin' way. He'd been preoccupied at the time, dealing with his own angst over his injured dog.

The memory of his dog brought a quick smile. "My pal, Snoop. Best dog ever." He'd been so scared, but good ole' Doc. Gates had fixed his pal, and a silly, young Sam had hid under a pine tree. Points for Sam, though, because when he'd told her about Snoop, she'd assured him her grandpa would fix everything, and she'd been dead on.

She'd stood up for her grandpa's skill as a vet, but showed no common sense by heading out unprepared in the middle of a frigging lake effect snow event.

Wind rocked his trusty truck. "Well, Deja' vu. She's not a kid anymore, but she's out here somewhere in the middle of a snow storm."

His truck's engine hummed louder as it started to climb, and he wrenched the wheel to stay on track. He cranked the defroster up another notch then straightened, gripping the wheel with both hands.

He could barely see ten feet ahead, and when his lights caught twin flashes of red, half on half off the narrow lane, he hit the brakes and slid to a stop.

He shoved the truck into reverse and tried to back away, but snow jammed beneath it blocked his retreat. "Come on, come on, damn it." Mike's hopes nosedived when the tires whined, and a steady thump, thump produced no backward movement. He shifted into park and tried the door. The angle, combined with the weight of his truck and the sudden dip when he'd braked had not only lodged snow beneath the front end, but as high as the window on the driver's side door.

He was trapped.

He shut off the engine, shoved aside his mom's whipped cream and climbed over the console to reach the opposite door. In the process, he cracked his elbow on the steering wheel and suffered a painful cramp in one leg, but he somehow managed to reach the passenger door and shove it open.

Snow smacked him in the face, and because of the angle the damn door wouldn't stay open. Mike used his feet, levered himself up, and dropped into the snow beside the truck. The door slammed shut, whacking him upside the head in the process. Slightly dazed, he slid down, leaning against the truck with his knees drawn up and his arms wrapped around them, staring into the wind-driven snow as the world turned from white to black.

Snow hitting his face brought him around. He took a deep breath, swallowing a rush of nausea. He removed one glove and gingerly touched his forehead. Blood coated his fingers and trickled down the side of his face.

"Great, just great."

Besides a possible concussion, he was hungry and his left elbow hurt like a son-of-a-bitch,

"Well, happy frickin' holidays," he muttered.

He took a second to catch his breath and still his pounding heart before he struggled to his feet. He peered through the blinding snow. He blinked, trying to focus on those twin flashes of red he'd seen before he ditched the truck, and the bleary outline of a large SUV emerged. Unfortunately, it was leaning like a drunk into the bank on the left hand side of the road.

The vehicle had to be Sam's. But where was she? *How* was she? There was no movement, no hand waving to acknowledge his arrival. There was no sign of life or tracks exiting the vehicle.

His own injuries forgotten, Mike yanked open the door of his truck and reached behind the seat, dragging out the emergency pack he always carried. He checked the contents, first aid kit, and extra clothes along with solar blanket, and a cache of energy bars. He retrieved his service revolver, tucked it into the holster at his waist and then slung the pack over his shoulder. Just as he was about to slam the door, he remembered his soft-sided pack. He'd tossed jeans, a sweatshirt and shaving gear into it, along with a nice sweater and trousers, planning to leave it at his mom's. He'd planned, as always, to spend the night Christmas Eve and his mom was a stickler about everyone looking decent at her Christmas dinner table. He could be a slob all morning during the package ripping, but come dinner time he'd better appear clean shaven and wearing something presentable.

That's the way it had always been, and he was pleased the tradition had stuck all these years. Although he wouldn't admit it and always whined and complained until she threatened. A ritual they both understood and laughed about each year.

He shivered, and pushed thoughts of past holiday traditions aside. Daylight was fading fast, faster than usual due to the overcast sky and falling snow. He leaned against his truck as a fresh wave of nausea washed over him.

"Damn it, I don't have time for this now." He closed his eyes, waiting until he felt steady, then lashed the two packs together, secured them on his shoulder and called out," Sam. Samantha, can you hear me?"

Only the snap of bare branches slapping together high above answered him over the driving wind. He moved forward, trying not to stagger like a damn drunk. He skirted the rear of Sam's SUV and bent to peer inside.

A queasy mix of relief and fear stirred in his gut when he found the vehicle empty. He straightened, called out again, and then froze. A faint sound rose above the wind, and his blood ran cold. He yanked his hood aside, listening, and settled his hand on the butt of the gun at his waist as a wolf's eerie call filled the air.

*****

Sam stumbled, her knees like jelly. She'd managed to cover about ten maybe fifteen feet struggling with the injured moose. Her breath came is short gasps and she tightened her grip on the scarf wrapped around the gangly, injured animal. The moose's wound still leaked blood like a faucet. Its raw, heavy scent almost gagged her as thick, red trails trickled down and dripped into the snow. She had no clue from which direction the wild call had come.

Then the unmistakable, haunting wail came again. There weren't supposed to be wolves in this part of the state.

There weren't supposed to be moose either, but here she was struggling to get one that had appeared out of nowhere to her grandfather's barn.

Had she stumbled into some weird animal black hole?

Her gaze swung left, then right, searching the gloomy forest around her. She steadied the shaky moose and peered back toward her Pilot. Her pulse thudded in her ears. Something came at her through the swirling snow, moving at a steady pace.

The moose grunted, ears erect, as his huge head swung toward the approaching threat.

Heart hammering, Sam shouted, "Get out! Go away!" Her voice squeaked, but she forced herself to stand tall and wave her free hand. All her training had taught her 'appear fearless, big and threatening in a cougar or bear encounter.' Like a mantra, she chanted the litany to herself and prayed it worked with wolves.

"Sam. Calm the hell down."

The clipped command cut through the screaming wind. The shadow became a person and Sam blew out a shaky breath, squinting as the shape materialized into human form and waded through hip deep snow toward her.

The moose shifted, and she almost went down. It leaned against her, and she called out, "Whoever you are, get over here and help me before this damn moose falls down again."

Chapter Five

Mike sprang forward. The moose lunged and he grabbed the scarf wrapped around the animal's neck. "I've got him."

Sam disappeared behind the moose's chunky body.

"Damn, it," Mike muttered, but seconds later, a gloved hand slapped onto the animal's back and Sam's face appeared. "Take my hand," she ordered.

Mike switched the scarf from one hand to the other, latched onto her wrist and pulled. She flopped her other arm onto the moose's back and hung there panting. "Thanks," she gasped, and Mike burst out laughing.

Her eyes went to icy blue slits. "What's so funny?"

The fur-rimmed hood of her parka had slid forward and only a small section of Sam's face was visible. Her brows were covered with snow and her nose was red as Rudolph's.

"I repeat, what's so darned funny?" She lifted her free hand and swiped at her face. Tiny flecks of ice flew from her frozen brows.

Mike steadied the wobbly moose and leaned down, nose to nose with Sam. Her chin barely reached the back of the moose. "I don't remember the last time I saw you, Sam, but it seems every time I do you're in deep shit of your own making. You look like you ran face first into a snowbank." He couldn't hold back the grin. "This time I think we're both in deep shit."

"Mike? Mike Donovan, is that you?"

"How'd you guess?"

A smile, close to a smirk, tipped her lips at the corners. "I'd recognize that toothy grin anywhere."

Mike clamped his mouth shut. She was still a smart ass. After all this time, knowing the crooked incisor he'd had all his life had given him away irked him.

A long, drawn out howl brought back stark reality.

Mike tightened his grip on the makeshift sling around the moose's neck. "Let's get the hell inside."

Sam gave a curt nod. "I had him moving. With your help I think we can make it to the garage. There's a barn attached in the rear. If we can get him in there, I can assess his wounds and maybe stop the bleeding. Speaking of bleeding, there's dried blood on your face."

Mike touched his forehead and winced, hoping like hell he'd not pass out halfway to that garage. "Yeah, yeah, it's nothing. Do you have keys?"

"Yes. They're in my backpack. I --"

Her head whipped around and she pushed her hood back. Her blue eyes a stark contrast to her chalk white skin. "That sounded closer. There aren't supposed to be wolves around here, Mike. Or moose," she said, glancing at their quivering patient as the wail faded.

"No shit," Mike muttered. "I can explain the moose, but you're right, that's definitely a wolf, and I'm as dumbstruck as you about where the hell it came from."

He met her wide-eyed gaze over the moose's back, adjusted the packs digging into his shoulder. "You steady him on your side, I'll see if I can get him moving. It's downhill to the garage and in our favor."

Once they reached the long, low building, they were sheltered a bit from the driving wind. Sam slid her pack off and dug out the key for the main door beside the large overhead.

She shoved the door open and ducked inside, slapping at light switches as she crossed the large open space and unlocked yet another door. Out of the driving wind, an illusion of warmth surrounded them as she helped Sam guide the injured animal into a roomy box stall in the attached barn. The scent of earth and straw permeated the inside of the barn, and the moose's hooves thudded on rough wood floors. As if he understood, the moose lurched forward into the stall and collapsed onto the floor.

Sam slid out of her bulky coat. "Secure the doors," she ordered.

"Already done."

She gave a curt nod and moved about the room outside the stall gathering a large drape, white cloths from a chest and an assortment of instruments from various drawers.

Kneeling by the prone moose, with gentle, steady movements she eased the injured leg aside and spread the drape on the floor of the stall before gently placing the leg on it. Drops of blood marred the pristine white cloth.

Mike dropped the packs he carried. His vision blurred and he bent over, hands on his knees. After the sudden wave of nausea and dizziness passed, he stood, gazing around as he loosened his coat. There were two stalls along one wall. On the opposite wall were cabinets, a sink and counter, and a large metal table with wheels.

"Is this some kind of satellite office for your grandpa?"

Sam glanced up. "Not officially. He spends a lot of time here in the summer and..." From her kneeling position she eased back, resting on the heels of her feet.

"And," Mike prompted, getting a good look at her features unencumbered for the first time. A sprinkling of freckles trailed over the bridge of her nose. Her skin, the color of light cream, contrasted with tangled hair the color of rich mahogany.

25

"And, it's where I first learned how to care for injured wild animals. Grandpa loves caring for pets, dogs and cats, but he gets a lot of satisfaction helping wild creatures. I suspect, no," she insisted, "I *know* without his help many wouldn't have survived."

The moose heaved a deep, shuddering sigh.

Sam's attention sharpened on the animal, and as she leaned closer to examine his wound, she called over her shoulder, "There's a gas stove by the sink. There should be matches in a box on the shelf above it. Light a burner and get some water from the pump. Once you've done that, see if you can get a fire started in the wood burner in the corner. It should be stocked and ready. It'll at least take the chill off."

Feeling steadier, Mike moved to do what she'd asked. Regular water lines would be shut off in the unheated building, but a hand pump tapped into a spring or well was... friggin' ingenious.

He detoured first and dug into one of his own packs, retrieving a solar blanket. Returning to the stall, he attempted to drape the blanket over Sam's shoulders.

"What the... Oh, a solar blanket. Good thinking." She grinned up at him. "Thanks."

He bit back his objection when she shrugged it off and rose to tuck it around the shivering moose. Could be he'd underestimated the woman the air-headed girl had become.

"I'll need warm water and antiseptic wash," Sam said, kneeling close to the injured leg. She hunched her shoulders and tucked her hands beneath her arms.

God, her fingers must be freezing. His were.

"You'll find everything in those cupboards." She nodded toward the opposite wall.

Mike fired up a burner and, locating a large pan filled it with water from the pump and put it on to heat. He lit the kindling and rubbed his hands over the sputtering flame as it caught and began to burn.

"Make sure the flue is open," Sam called out.

"I'm not an idiot," he shot back. Then clamped his mouth shut. Just because his head throbbed like a beating drum was no reason to act like a jerk on top of everything. She was being a bit bossy, though.

He rummaged through well labeled cupboards stocked with supplies. When steam rose from the simmering pot, he filled a shallow metal bowl and grabbed liquid antiseptic soap, along with other items she'd requested, and returned to the stall.

With quick, efficient moves, Sam arranged everything beside her. "I don't know how he's going to react. It's bound to hurt. He's lost a lot of blood and he's weak. God, I hope it's not too late," she murmured, delivering a gentle stroke along his neck. She sucked in a deep breath, rolled her shoulders." I'll need your help," she said. "Get on the other side of him and kneel down. I hope you won't have to physically restrain

26

him. Try to keep him calm. Talk to him."

Mike dropped into position. "*Talk* to him?"

Her brow furrowed. "You heard me. He's used to human voices, a human's touch."

"How the hell do you know that?"

"You must think I'm an idiot," she snapped. "Well, I'm not."

Mike clamped his mouth shut. He'd been on the verge of asking what he should say to a moose, but there was no sense being a smart ass and pissing her off.

Frowning, Sam added antiseptic to the warm water. "Just say a little prayer he doesn't kick the heck out of us," she muttered. She dribbled some treated water into her palms, rubbed them together and then dried them on one of the soft white clothes. "Not as good as a full scrub up, but I can't take the time."

She refocused on the moose, and Mike shifted, trying to ignore the cold floor beneath his butt.

As she cleaned blood from the ragged wound, Sam talked in a quiet, steady voice. "As to your doubts about my knowledge, or my ability, here's something to think about. This moose is a six or seven month old male. By six months they easily weigh four hundred pounds. I'd say this guy is older, closer to seven or eight months. So, add another hundred pounds. He may have started out wild, but I suspect for at least the past few months he wasn't on his own. If he'd been totally wild, we'd never have been able to handle him."

She paused, gave Mike a sharp look. "Are you all right? You're white as the darned snow."

"I'm fine. What next?"

"I'm going to irrigate the wound with a strong antiseptic. Be alert. Five hundred pounds of hurting moose can be dangerous."

Mike stroked a tentative hand over the animal's long neck. She shot him a withering look. "For Pete's sake, Mike, he's a moose, not a damn poodle," she snapped out, and then gave him a wry grin. "Come to think of it, *I* had to get stitches the first time I helped Grandpa with a damn poodle."

Mike figured her confession arose from a need to ease tension between them, just as her brief lesson on 'moose facts' was meant to put him in his place for questioning her ability. She'd tactfully managed to do both.

So he put more effort into his comforting strokes and kept any further doubts to himself. Though it made him feel just plain weird, he began to talk softly to the moose. She needed all the help she could get.

His experience with wildlife was more along the lines of control and protection. He'd been around wild animals, mostly deer or small mammals, all part of his job. On occasion there'd been injuries, but they'd

27

been minor up till now and he'd managed. Determined to hold up his end he followed Sam's directions.

As he observed her competent moves, he admitted that his skills were nowhere close to hers, and without a doubt, the stubborn, silly girl he'd known all those years ago had changed.

Warmth from the stove began to spread as they knelt on the hard floor, and the antiseptic smell of the products Sam used overrode the stable's earthy scent.

Chapter Six

Sam sat back on her heels. Her hands, palms up, lay limp on her thighs. The poor animal was so weak he'd done no more that quiver and moan as she'd cleaned and taped his wound. A mixed blessing.

She met Mike's gaze over the prone moose. "That wound should have been stitched, but I just didn't want to take the time. Too much risk." She rubbed her nose with the back of her hand. "At least the bleeding has stopped."

"He lost a lot of blood."

"He did," Sam agreed, and shoved to her feet. She used what was left of the heated water to scrub off dried blood. Her hands shook as she dried them.

Mike approached. "I'd say there's not much more we can do now but wait."

"I'd like to rig an IV."

"Can you do that?"

Sam bit back the urge to remind him *again* that she wasn't an idiot. "I can, but I'm not going to. I wouldn't want to leave him with a drip going. I need to get into the cabin and warm up. My hands are freezing."

Mike pulled off his gloves stuffed them into his pockets. He reached out, took her hands and folded them between his. "Mine aren't much better, but at least I had gloves on."

Sam closed her eyes, absorbing the pure bliss of shared warmth.

When she opened them her gaze locked with Mike's. Her heart gave a jump. Clear green eyes stared down at her, and a dark scruff, the exact color of his deep coppery hair, shadowed his lower face. He was being nice, and now *she* felt like an idiot for snapping at him and for the crooked tooth remark. "I'm sorry. I didn't mean to insult you."

A frown creased Mike's brow, drawing her attention to the dried blood on his forehead.

"What do you mean?"

Ignoring his question, Sam pulled her hands from his grasp and took a firm hold of his chin with one hand. She pushed his hair back, revealing a nasty gash.

He jerked. "Hey, that hurts."

"Don't be a baby. Get over here," she demanded and grasped his arm and pulled him forward. "Stay right here."

She relit the gas burner and refilled the water container. Glancing around she spied a stool and dragged it to where they stood. "Sit. I'm going to clean that gash on your head. How'd you get it, anyway?"

Easing onto the stool, Mike loosened his jacket. "The damn door hit me. I ditched my truck in order to avoid your Pilot and had to climb out the passenger door. The angle was steep, and when the wind caught the truck's door I got smacked on the head." He rubbed his arm. "I bashed my elbow climbing over the console, too."

"Oh, poor baby. I'll look at that once I see if your head needs stitching."

He straightened. Male alarm and denial streaked over his face. "You wouldn't take a chance stitching a damn moose. You're sure as hell not practicing on my head."

Sam tested the water. "I don't practice. Now *you're* insulting me."

"We'll explore the 'whys' of insults later." He started to get up.

"Sit down. All I'm going to do is clean your injury. Or do you want to risk infection when we may be stuck out here for God knows how long?" She dipped a cloth in the simmering pan of water. "Now hold still, and try not to cry like a baby."

With careful strokes, she dabbed and worked the dried blood from the gash on Mike's head. It wasn't as bad as she'd feared once the blood was removed. She retrieved some butterfly bandages and, after easing the edges of the nasty gash together, smoothed them into place.

"There, that will hold you for a while." Once more she gripped his chin. "Hold still, I want to look into your eyes."

Mike grinned. "Well, darlin', I'm flattered," he drawled.

She drew back, gave his cheek a little pat. "Don't be, I just want to make sure you don't have a concussion."

She moved away to dump the water and toss the soiled cloth, putting some distance between them. Her reaction to his charming grin and looking into those intense green eyes threw her. The man wasn't blind. It also appeared he had a bit of an ego, and Sam didn't want to send the wrong message or encourage him.

Mike stoked the wood burner while she checked on her patient.

"He's so still." She knelt and ran a hand over his neck. His eyes fluttered, but remained closed. Slow and steady, his side rose and fell beneath Mike's solar blanket.

Satisfied for now, she pushed to her feet. "I'll keep checking on him. That's all I can do for now." She dug out a key. They gathered the packs they'd dumped upon entering the barn and she led the way through an enclosed breezeway into the cabin. The heat was set low inside the rustic building, probably no more than fifty-five degrees. But when they stepped inside, it felt like a sauna compared to the chilly barn.

****

Mike sat on a bench inside the door and leaned down to remove his boots. He bolted to his feet when Sam squealed. "What the hell?" He was half way across the room before he realized the sound she'd made was excitement, not shock or panic. He stopped, grasping the back of a chair as the room spun.

"Look. Look, Mike. Grandpa brought the Christmas tree inside and it's all ready to decorate." She turned to him, eyes glowing. "He's so smart. He *knew* we'd get a storm and thought ahead." She fumbled in her pockets. "I want to call him," she said, then frowned. "My cell. I can't find my cell." She hurried to where she'd tossed her jacket. "Maybe it's here, or... darn, I bet I left it in the Pilot."

Steadier now, Mike stepped in front of her as she shrugged into her jacket and headed for the door. "Whoa, hold on, Sam. You can't go out there in this mess. Plus, did you forget about what we heard?"

His mind raced. He had to tell her about her grandfather. With the storm, the moose, and all the other crap he'd been dealing with, he'd totally forgotten about her grandpa's trip to the ER.

She zipped her coat, glaring up at him. "It's not that far, and if it will make you feel better I'll take Grandpa's rifle."

"You know how to handle a rifle?"

"Now *you're* insulting me. I'm not like the girls who chased after you in high school."

"What? What girls?"

Pain made it hard to focus, and the room titled as he struggled to block her path to the door. She scooted around him. Before she reached for the door, Mike managed to gain his balance and hooked his arm around her waist. He lifted her off her feet and pulled her back into the room. Her heels smacked against his shins.

"Ouch. Damn it, Sam. Quit wiggling like a dam fish on a hook. You're kicking me."

"Put me down, or I'll do worse than kick you."

"Okay, enough of this shit. I have your cell phone."

Sam froze.

He set her down and removed his arm. "Let's sit down," he said, "before I fall down."

He ran his hands up her arms. Gripping her shoulders, he turned her to face him.

Her gaze swept over his face. "Something's wrong."

He steered her to the long low sofa in front of the fireplace. "Take off your coat and sit," he ordered.

"I'm sorry. I forgot about your head."

"My head's not the issue here, Sam." He sighed and, frowning, she eased onto the sofa.

Her pretty blue eyes filled as he relayed what he knew about

31

Charley Gates and how he'd come to find her cell. "Your phone came on at first, but the screen was smashed and after a few tries it went dead."

"What about yours? We can use yours, call the hospital."

"We can try, but with this weather I doubt we'll succeed."

Sam stood and swiped at her moist cheeks. "We have to try. Where's your phone?"

For a moment, his mind went blank. Where was the damn thing? "It should be in my coat pocket." He rose and checked, going through every compartment, twice, and then snapped his fingers. "That's it. I tried to use it just before I turned off the main road. There was no signal, so I tossed it onto the console." He touched the throbbing gash on his head. "God knows where it ended up when I landed in the ditch."

Sam's brows lifted. "Are you sure you're all right?"

"I'm fine, but I know what you're thinking, and the answer is no."

"Why? It's not like your truck is ten miles away, and you have a gun," she added, pointing at the weapon strapped on his hip.

"Samantha, use your head. We're both exhausted. I'm fine," he repeated, "but I'm starved and not quite warm all the way through yet." He glanced around. "Let's get a fire going. If your grandpa brought a tree inside, I'll bet he stocked up on some food, too. We need to refuel, rest."

Sam's shoulders slumped. Dark circles beneath her eyes stood out against her pale skin. "You're right. I could use some food, too. It's just that..."

She covered her face with both hands. Mike gritted his teeth. He wasn't good with weeping women, but he went to her and pulled her into his arms, holding her until her sobs subsided.

"I'm sorry." She eased away.

"No need to apologize. I'm sorry I had such bad news."

Her eyes filled again.

Shit.

"How about I scrounge for food and you check on your patient?" He started to walk away, then turned and looked straight at her. "And for the love of God, Sam, don't go behind my back and do something stupid. If anything happened to you I have no clue on how to take care of an injured moose. Go, do what needs to be done," he ordered, figuring if he gave her something to distract and redirect her focus it might take the edge off, give her time to settle.

She drew in a shaky breath and nodded, but the stubborn set of her chin didn't go unnoticed as she slipped her coat on. The door snapped shut behind her and he winced, and then went in search of food.

*****

Sam pulled gloves from her pockets and yanked them on. All right darn it, she'd take a step back, refuel and do what had to be done to please Mr. Sensible Donovan.

She checked the young moose and banked straw around him. No visible changes, a good sign overall. The barn seemed a bit warmer, and she added fuel to the woodstove. Every bone in her body ached. The spot along her ribs where the seatbelt had caught her throbbed. Lightheadedness and nausea plagued her. She paused, taking one last look at her patient and discovered that doing what needed to be done had helped settle her.

She was still tired. Exhausted, actually, but more focused. Not as frantic as she'd been when Mike told her about Grandpa. She choked out a laugh. She owed him. If he hadn't come after her she'd be here dealing with an injured moose and she wouldn't even know about Grandpa.

Outside the wind howled, rattling the back door. She shivered. Was it only the wind? Knowing a wolf lurked somewhere out there chilled her to the core. *Not* knowing how Grandpa was squeezed her heart.

The last time they'd talked Grandma had told her Grandpa had a touch of indigestion. "Don't worry," she'd said, and promised they'd arrive the next day, but Sam was well aware that indigestion was a red flag, a warning sign of a heart attack.

Would her grandparents be here to trim the tree with her on Christmas Eve?

Tears welled, and she sucked in a deep breath. Crying never solved anything, she'd learned that early in life, and it embarrassed her to think Mike had seen her lose it.

He'd held her, comforted her until she'd pulled it together. Strong arms, hard body. Nothing like the scrawny kid she remembered with the cute, crooked toothed smile that had twisted her pre-teen self into knots all those years ago.

She'd die before she'd ever admit to the painful crush she'd had on him back then. A lot of girls had *adored* Mike Donovan's shy little smile. She wasn't a teenager anymore, and her recent reaction to that smile packed a dangerous punch.

The door to the house opened. "Everything all right out there?"

"Yes, his condition is about the same."

"Come on back inside, then. I struck pay dirt on food."

"I'll be right there."

A tempting aroma enveloped her as she reentered the cabin. She swallowed hard, fighting the lump in her throat that wouldn't go away, hoping whatever she forced down wouldn't come right back up and embarrass her even more than her uncontrollable tears had done.

*****

Mike ladled hot soup into deep bowls. "I found this in a big container in the fridge. I think its vegetable beef."

Sam sniffed the air and broke into a smile. "Grandma's special recipe." She removed her coat and hung it by the door. "I need to wash up and change. I'll be right back."

She grabbed her duffle and disappeared down a narrow hall to the bathroom where before warming the soup he'd washed up and checked his injury. She'd done a nice job patching him up.

The soup bubbled away, and damn it smelled good. Tearing a hunk from the loaf of bread he'd discovered, he dipped it into the soup and popped it into his mouth. "Mmm... tastes as good as it smells."

He blew out a long breath and as he stirred the soup, stared out the window over the sink.

What a friggin' mess.

They were isolated. Alone together in a remote cabin two days before Christmas trapped by a raging lake effect storm that showed no sign of letting up any time soon.

Every year he looked forward to Christmas with his family, his mom's traditional baked ham, his dad's spiked eggnog. All his friends, many he didn't see much anymore, would drop by. His best buddy Al might be a daddy by then, his sister a mom. Sharing that new phase in their life on that first Christmas... well, it doesn't get much better.

He glanced down the silent hallway. What was taking her so long? He sucked at handling weepy women, and if she was in there crying again... well, she'll just have to get a grip.

A door closed and footsteps headed his way.

She'd cleaned up and pulled her hair back from her face. The bulky layers of clothes were gone. A soft looking, deep blue sweater clung to generous curves, and jeans tucked into low boots hugged endless legs.

He froze mid stir and his mind emptied.

She stopped, staring at him, and then glanced down at herself. "Is something wrong?"

Mike blinked. "No, sorry. I just... you never..."

For the first time since their bizarre adventure began, she smiled. Really smiled and walked to him. "I quit imitating fashion models a while back, Mike, and much to my mother's dismay, blossomed late in life. I imagine your first memory was a skinny tomboy, and then later on, the shapeless fashion model I was encouraged to portray."

He didn't get the model reference, but she'd sure as hell blossomed. "Except for the incident under the tree, I only saw you a few times,, Sam."

She frowned. "Tree?"

To keep from gawking like an awestruck teen, he turned back to the soup. "Yeah, I met you under a big pine tree. Funny," he mused, "there was a snowstorm that day, too." He tapped the spoon on the pan. "Snoop, my dog was hurt and — "

"Grandpa helped him," she broke in and came to stand beside him. "I was mad at my parents because I couldn't be with my grandparents for Christmas."

"You came that year, though. I remember my dad telling me how his friend Charley, your grandpa, got his way."

She reached into a cupboard beside the stove. "Grandpa made a deal with my mom and dad. He could be sneaky to get his way."

Mike winced when she bit her lip. Please, God, no tears.

"Whatever he did, it worked," he said as she opened a drawer for spoons. "My dad missed seeing yours over the holidays. They'd been close growing up. Your family came at Christmas for years, but after that year, I can't remember the next time we saw your parents."

Sam placed the bowls beside the bubbling pot. "They made a deal that year. I'm not sure what leverage Grandpa used, but Mom agreed I could always come for Christmas." She smiled as she ladled soup into each bowl, and then carried them to the long wooden table across the room. "It worked, and I have wonderful memories of all those years."

"It must have been hard for them, your parents I mean, not to have you spend the holidays with them."

"No, I'd say it was a relief. All those parties, all the quote, 'social obligations of professionals' unquote, they didn't have to feel guilty about attending and leaving me with a sitter."

Mike bent and pulled two bottles of water from the fridge. He handed one to Sam. "But as you got older, weren't you included in the parties? Maybe with a date." He twisted the top off his water and sipped.

Sam slid onto a chair. "I was expected to appear very lady like and proper. My mom's dreams, that look, not mine. In high school I couldn't stand the snobs she wanted me to cultivate as friends. Girls with nicknames like Kiki and Cookie. Guys called Biff."

Mike burst out laughing, nearly choking on his water. "But didn't everyone call you Sam?"

"No, in front of Mom no one dared call me Sam. It was always Samantha. Only when we were alone did Dad let it slip. But when I came home to Watertown, everyone called me Sam. They still do. Eat your soup before it gets cold. "

He settled across the table from her. As they spooned up hot soup, Mike figured there was a lot he didn't know about the little girl from his past, the woman she'd become, and the journey between the two, and he decided he wanted to learn more.

Outside driven snow pounded the cabin. Mike's eyes drooped. His arms and legs grew heavy. He turned to Sam. "You look exhausted."

Sam pushed her bowl aside, sipped some water. She'd finished her first bowl, but when he'd refilled his, she'd declined. A half-eaten slice of bread lay by her empty bowl.

"I am tired. But, Mike, I'm afraid to close my eyes. I keep picturing Grandpa lying in a hospital bed."

Mike rose and carried his bowl and spoon to the sink. "Try not to imagine the worst. You need to keep up your strength, Sam. There's nothing we can do until this storm ends except keep our friend out there as comfortable as possible. I know I feel better with some food in my gut. Too bad there are no twigs and leaves handy to feed the poor guy. Sit," he ordered when Sam moved to clear her spot at the table. He scooped up her bowl and spoon.

She slid her chair back from the table. "There's a root cellar at the rear of the barn with dried fruit and veggies for Al."

"Al? And he'll eat fruit and vegetables?"

"Yes, Al. It seems stupid to keep calling him the patient, or the moose. Alces alces is the scientific name for moose, and he's a member of the deer family, cervidae. I learned that when I worked at a sanctuary in Canada, and, yes, that's what we fed the moose. I'm concerned about getting liquid into him, too."

Mike rinsed the two bowls and spoons as they talked. Sam's eyes drooped, and her whole body appeared to slump where she sat.

"Sam, go stretch out on the sofa. You don't have to sleep, just rest. Are there any Advil or Tylenol, or something around here?" His head ached, and the place where he'd gotten whacked by the door throbbed like a bitch. If she'd just settle, even for an hour, he could try and get off his feet and regroup.

She went to a cupboard next to the sink, opened the door and reached inside. "Here you go."

He nearly wept with gratitude when she handed him the familiar blue and white Advil container, and washed two down with the remainder of his water. "Do you need one? You said your ribs hurt."

When he got no reply, he glanced around. She'd disappeared. He started for the door. "Damn it, Sam, if you've--"

Then he stopped, and the tension drained from his body like syrup. He crossed the room and silently draped a thick, knitted throw over Sam's prone body. She lay on the sofa in front of the fireplace, curled on her side with her head cradled on folded hands, sound asleep.

Moving as quietly as possible, he added logs to the fire. Daylight was fading, so he turned on a lamp in the corner, not wanting her to wake in the dark. He eyed a hefty, overstuffed recliner on the other side of the room. Locating another throw, he settled down, tilted back and was out like a light within seconds.

Chapter Seven

Sam awoke in stages. She snuggled beneath a warm throw as the fire simmered and hissed. Hot coals glowed, but aside from a small lamp in one corner, the room was shrouded in darkness.

Where was Mike?

She stretched, repositioned on the ancient sofa and winced when her sore ribs protested. The wind didn't sound as forceful, but it was hard to tell without getting up and looking outside. At the moment, doing so sounded way too ambitious.

Suddenly, a loud, thump and bang came from behind the door leading to the barn. Sam tossed the throw aside and swung her feet to the floor. She paused, listening. In her half-awake state, maybe it was just her imagination.

There it was again. This time the thumping was accompanied by guttural grunts and one sharp cry.

Fumbling in the dark, Sam searched for her coat and boots. She slipped on her coat and tugged on the boots. Staggering a bit, she crossed the room, yanked open the door and raced through the walkway. They'd left the light on in the barn and closed the entry to the stall. She crossed to the sliding wooden partition and shoved it open.

The spot where they'd left the injured moose was empty. Her gaze swept the enclosed space. "Easy fella," she crooned when the dark outline of her patient materialized against the back wall of the stall. He swung his head toward her, the whites of his eyes flashed.

She stepped closer, easing the stall's door shut behind her. The bad thing was there wasn't enough light to tell if he'd ripped open his leg. The good thing was he'd been strong enough to get to his feet.

His breath came in rapid pants, visible in the cool air. She closed the distance between them. When less than two feet away, she realized they were almost eye to eye. Much taller, and, she had to admit, a bit scarier than the weak, crumpling animal she'd helped through hip high drifts.

"I bet you're thirsty, big guy. If you let me check your leg, I'll buy you a drink. How's that sound?"

"Sounds like you've lost your frickin mind." Mike's deep voice came from behind her. "Are you crazy, woman?"

"Get a bucket and fill it with water."

"Yes, ma am," Mike retorted, sarcasm heavy in his voice.

"Please."

His footsteps moved away. A moment later the pump creaked, followed by the splash of water.

She kept her eyes aimed at the moose, talking nonsense hoping to keep him from rushing her. Her sturdy one-twenty-five was no match for a five hundred pound moose.

The stable door creaked and she felt rather than heard Mike approach. The moose's gaze shifted up and over. He stretched his neck, testing the air.

Mike tapped her left shoulder and she reached down and grasped the handle of the bucket he passed to her. Slow and careful, holding her breath, she lifted the bucket.

Nostrils set deep in the oversized moose nose flared. He stretched his neck, Sam inched forward. Better to take the water to him and not risk him faltering and falling on his injured leg, or worse, on her.

"Here you go, Al." When the huge head lowered and the moose began to drink, Sam shot a quick grin at Mike over her shoulder. "Quit frowning, grumpy. Do I know moose talk or what?"

She let Al drink. He paused at times, blinking at her, sending long slow looks at Mike. "That's enough, big guy," she said finally, and lowered the bucket. "A little at a time is best."

Easing back to the stall's entry, she glanced at Mike. "I'm going to check out the root cellar. I know there's always some stuff there. I can chop it up fine and try to get some into him." When Mike didn't reply, she gave him a hard look.

He had his arms crossed, resting on the top of the stall. His head rested on his crossed arms.

"Mike?"

He looked up, blinked. "Yeah, I heard you." He straightened. "Point me in the right direction and I'll help you with Al's dinner."

She noted his hands still gripped the top rail of the stall. "I can handle it. I'll just put some in the stall for him. He did okay with the water, I'm hoping he'll go for the food, too."

Mike only nodded.

"Mike, I can handle things out here. Why don't you go back inside and take it easy."

"I'm--"

"I know, you're fine, but before I switched to veterinary I was pre-med. I think the blow you took was harder than you think. A concussion is nothing to ignore."

"I don't think I have a concussion, I'm just beat. You're sure you can handle things here?"

"I'm sure. I am getting hungry again, though. Could you heat up some of Grandma's soup for us?"

"No problem," Mike said, and headed for the cabin.

The root cellar held a trove of goodies, apples, carrots and more. No surprise there. Her grandparents were like pack rats when it came to stocking up for winter days at the cabin.

38

She located a knife and chopped everything fine. Instead of a pan or dish, Sam hunted up a flat piece of board and piled the moose dinner on top of it. At least she *hoped* it would be a moose dinner.

Al was once more lying down, but in a more upright position, not flat on his side, and appeared more alert.

"Here you go, big fella." She slid the board within reach, stepped back and closed the stall door.

He stretched his neck, sniffed. His gaze lifted and he seemed to study her.

"Okay, I'll leave you alone."

She checked the wood burner, stoked it, and, leaving a small light burning, left Al to his dinner and returned to the cabin.

Mike was stirring the soup as she entered, and its heavenly smell filled the room. She slipped out of her coat and toed her boots off. "Well, there's food in front of him. Now it's up to Al."

She turned to hang up her jacket.

The clatter of a spoon hitting the floor made her whip around, just in time to see Mike slide to the floor like slow moving molasses.

*****

The scent tickled his glands. Something sweet, like vanilla, tangled with pure woman. Eyes closed, he wrapped his arms around her. Warmth chased the chill. From close by the crackle of burning logs filled the air, but fireplace heat wasn't what sent his temperature soaring.

Unaware, Mike rolled and pulled her tight against him.

"Hey. Hey, let go of me."

The more hands pushed against him and that soft body wiggled against him, the less he wanted to let go. Caught in that hazy state between awareness and oblivion, Mike wanted to dive in and ride the lazy, sensual wave.

"Mike. Mike, please."

Clawing his way to consciousness, her plea echoed in his head. A hand snaked up and firmly cupped his cheek. Forcing his eyes open took supreme effort, but through emerging slits, his foggy gaze focused on soft lips, smooth skin and freckled cheeks.

Flames danced in clear blue eyes inches from his.

His eyes flew open, and he realized the sweet smelling woman he'd locked in a very compromising embrace was Sam. He hoped like hell the flames in her eyes were the reflection of the blazing fireplace at his back and not simmering anger.

He blinked, figured 'why not' and kissed her. At first, she stiffened. Then with a sigh she softened and kissed him right back.

At this point Mike was well aware of whom he was kissing, but he

39

had no idea how in the hell he'd ended up lying on the floor in front of the fireplace pressed against the curvy, inviting body of Samantha Gates.

He loosened his grip, scrutinizing her expression in the glow of firelight. Was she going to kiss him again or haul off and clock him upside the head?

Her gaze roamed over his face, her hand rubbed his cheek. "You've got some five o'clock shadow," she observed. "And, from what just happened, I guess you're feeling better."

He grinned. "I can attest to feeling better. I have no clue how I managed to get here, but I'm in no hurry to leave."

Her gaze focused on his lips, hopeful possibilities raced through his foggy brain. Then she sighed and eased away, settling on one bent arm. "You passed out. Over there," she added, tilting her head toward the kitchen.

"No way."

"Yes, way, and I dragged you over here by the fireplace. For God's sake, Mike, how much do you weigh? You look tall and lanky, but you're solid as a rock."

He blew out a slow breath and did a cautious readjustment. "You have no idea, Sam." He wasn't sure if she got the implied message and blushed or if the fire flushed her cheeks.

Averting her eyes, she pushed up and settled back on her heels. "You scared me." She touched his injured forehead. "When you're steadier I want to take a look at your head again and check you over."

Mike flopped onto his back and folded one arm over his eyes. His head wasn't throbbing as bad as earlier, more a snare drum roll instead of a rock beat. "So I scared you, huh?"

"You kind of folded and slid down like oozing butter. I tried to bring you around, but you were out cold. Does light bother you?"

"Some." He lifted his arm, peering up at her. "I know. That's the sign of a concussion. So, you were right, Doctor Gates. What do we do now?"

"We wait, and watch. No lifting or doing anything to create pressure. You need to rest, but I'll wake you every couple of hours."

He rolled onto his side. "I guess that means you'll have to stay... close."

She gave him an inscrutable look. "For twenty-four hours you do little to nothing."

He gave her a noncommittal smile and decided changing the subject was wise. "How's Al, the moose?"

"My *other* patient was fine, last I checked. I don't know if he ate anything because I've been a little preoccupied."

He brushed her hand away when she moved to help him stand. Maybe the room tilted, just a little, but all in all he felt pretty good. "Did you turn off the soup?"

"I did," she said and hastened across the room, scooping up the spoon he'd dropped when he went down. "I can warm it again if you're hungry." She stepped to the sink to wash the spoon.

Mike moved to the table and sat. "Actually, I am. The nausea I've had off and on seems to have lessened."

"That's good. Still," she added, and turned the heat on under the soup. "You've got to eat small amounts and pay attention to how you feel."

True to her word, she only filled his bowl half full and did the same for hers. "You need to keep your strength up, too," he said, and grasped her hand when she placed the bowl in front of him without responding.

She looked at their joined hands, then into his eyes. "I'll be okay."

"You're beat, Sam. Today took a toll, physically and emotionally."

Her hand trembled. "It's not knowing, Mike. Grandpa could be..."

"Stop right there. He's a strong man, and he's being taken care of. Your grandma is with him. If you keep imagining all kinds of bad shit you'll tie yourself in knots." He released her hand and she sat down across from him. "Let's get through tonight. From the sounds of things, the wind hasn't let up, and last I looked it was still snowing like hell. First light I'll use those snowshoes I saw in the barn and get to my truck."

Sam's chin lifted, her shoulders squared. "If you can't, I will."

He scooped up some soup, nodded. "I think by morning I'll be fine. I know a little about concussions, too. If this was going to get worse, it would have by now."

"I'll still check on you throughout the night," she said, her blush unmistakable this time when he responded, "I'm counting on it."

*****

Sam cleaned up the kitchen and stored the soup. She noticed the fridge was fully stocked and ready for Christmas. The tangible evidence that Grandpa had recently been there made her heart ache. Where was Grandpa now?

How was he?

Christmas Eve was their special time, and it appeared the fates had joined forces to wreck everything. With her future plans still in flux, she had no idea when she'd have a chance to come for the holidays again.

Fate had also thrown her a curve by stranding her with Mike Donovan. When he'd kissed her she thought her head would explode.

The man knew how to kiss.

Guilt heated her cheeks, and she glanced across the room where Mike was stretched out on the sofa by the fireplace. Arms crossed, he gazed at the dancing flames.

His face shadowed with sexy stubble, his firm lips set in a stubborn line, and those intense green eyes were distractions she didn't need right

41

now. Her reaction to his kiss and being caught tight against Mike's *unmistakable* male body shocked her.

She'd had relationships with men. A few intimate encounters, but not one in the admittedly small numbers, shook her to the core like her brief encounter with Mike. She wouldn't even call it an encounter.

Yet.

She frowned, wet a sponge and began wiping off the counter. With his head injury she assumed the man wasn't up to par. If his reaction and the way he'd held her and kissed her weren't up to par, God help her when he was fully recovered.

"Hey, where's your mind wandered to?"

She turned from wiping the counter and almost smacked into him.

He took her shoulders, steadied her. "I asked you something, twice. You kept scrubbing the same spot on the counter as if you were in some kind of trance."

With his warm hands gripping her and his sleepy-eyed gaze searching her face, it was a wonder she didn't pool at his feet. He released his hold on her and stepped back. "Sam, it's time to shut it down for the night. Let's check on our moose and then get some sleep."

Thankful for the distraction, she placed the sponge aside and nodded, easing out of the danger zone. "Good idea."

Al was lying down, but lifted his head when they entered the barn.

"Look, Mike. He's eaten a bit."

"I'd say that's a good sign."

"It's a start."

Mike stood by while she entered the stall and offered more water, pleased when he drank and then settled into the straw without too much effort. His injury looked the same. No sign of more bleeding and the bandages were holding.

They stoked the woodstove, lowered the lights and returned to the cabin. While Mike banked the fire, Sam pondered their situation.

The cabin had two large bedrooms and a loft. She could sleep in her grandparents' room, but then she couldn't keep her eye on Mike. She paused outside the second bedroom. There were queen sized beds in each room and a double in the loft.

Guess she'd have to get creative. And, be strong.

"What are you doing?" Mike paused in the doorway of the second bedroom.

"I'm getting our bed ready."

"*Our*, bed?"

She straightened from forming a barrier with pillows, turned and smiled. "I'm not jumping up every couple of hours and running from room to room to check on you."

He studied her pillow barrier. Sam almost laughed when his hopeful expression dimmed.

He approached the bed. "Clever."

"I'm a clever woman, but I'm not made of stone." She turned and looked straight into his eyes. "Mike Donovan, you have a potent kiss."

"Right back at you, Samantha Gates."

A long moment passed, Sam looked away. She blew out a short breath. "I brought the alarm clock from my grandparents' room. I'll wake you every couple of hours and look at your eyes, check your alertness."

"My eyes, no problem there, but I feel it only fair to warn you more than my eyes will be alert."

Sam ignored his blatant implication and, as she left the room, called back at him, "I'll give you time to get... comfortable. I'm going to clean up and then I'll join you. Don't wait up."

When she returned, she was relieved to find him beneath the heavy quilt and already appeared to be sleeping. She'd changed into heavy sweats and slipped into bed on the opposite side of the pillow barrier as stealthy as a mouse beside a snoozing cat.

Her whole body sighed. The soft bed cradled her tired bones as she snuggled beneath the quilt they shared, a large quilt, thank goodness. It was late, close to eleven, so she'd set the alarm for one a.m. But as she began to drift off, the chilling howl they'd heard earlier rose above the wind.

She sunk deeper beneath the covers, listening. Wind buffeted the cabin, rattling the eaves. Once more the mournful cry rose, then fell and went silent. Sam glanced at Mike.

He lay on his side, facing her. His eyes were open, gleaming in light spilling from the hallway. "Yes, I heard it, too," he murmured. "We're safe, go to sleep, Sam."

He rolled over and pulled the covers up.

Sam turned her back on the sleeping man and stared at the illuminated hands on the alarm clock as the hours passed.

43

Chapter Eight

"Mike, wake up."

Her whisper, accompanied by a not so gentle shake brought an interesting dream to an abrupt halt.

"I'm awake," he mumbled, not opening his eyes. "And I'm fine. Now can I get back to..." Revealing his very vivid dream in which he was about to ravish his bedmate would be rude, and probably a bit provocative.

He scrubbed his hands over his face, wincing when he inadvertently hit his injury. "Okay, okay. Give me a minute."

"You don't have to get up, just look at me."

"Damn it," he yelped when he looked and she shined a tiny penlight right in his eyes.

"Hold still, and quit being such a baby. Look side to side, then up and down."

He did as she directed, trying not to squint. The room seemed chilly and he toyed with the idea of crawling out and throwing more fuel on the fire. "Are you warm enough?"

Sam had already tucked the light away and was resetting the clock. "As long as I stay under the covers I am. That wind hasn't let up and it's stripping the heat from the cabin." She slid down, pulled the covers up. "Go back to sleep. I'll check in a couple more hours. If you're all right then, I'll let you sleep on through till morning."

"I'm awake now. Maybe I should go stoke the fire."

"It's not necessary. Try to sleep, I haven't had much luck."

He turned facing her. Only the top of her head and her eyes peeked from beneath the quilt. "Quit thinking. It's the middle of the night and there's not a damn thing you can do until morning and the storm passes."

Her eyes closed. "I'll try. G'night." ·

Seconds later they opened again, a quick flash in the dim light spilling in from the hallway. With his eyes mere slits, Mike watched and waited.

Finally, he blew out a long breath. "I can't sleep with you not sleeping." Or with that sweet vanilla scent from whatever it was she used filling his head every time he inhaled.

"I'm sorry."

He folded his pillow, punched it into shape, and turned onto his back. After tugging the quilt up to his chin, he looked at her. "I could suggest something guaranteed to relax you."

When she raised one eyebrow and gave him a stone cold stare, he chuckled. "No? Okay, let's find something to talk about. Maybe you'll get bored and fall asleep."

Sam repositioned much the same as Mike until they both lay on their backs, heads elevated on pillows, staring at the ceiling. "I remember the first time I met you. Under the tree that winter," she began, "I was so mad at my parents."

"I saw you run out of your grandfather's house. No coat, no hat, but you sure as hell looked mad. Even from inside your grandpa's waiting room I could tell you were pissed. From that day forward, I only heard about you on occasion, though I saw you once in a while when you visited Watertown."

"I hated living in Boston, my mother loved it."

Mike angled his head to see her, surprised by her clipped response.

She glanced over, shrugged and refocused on the ceiling. "My dad, he was hard to read. He made a good living for us, but I think Mom's happiness played a big part in his feelings, one way or another."

"Happy wife, happy life?"

He detected a wry smile when she answered, "Something like that."

"But not a happy daughter."

"Not necessarily. Don't get me wrong, Mike, I had a good life. I just didn't measure up."

"Sam, how can you say that? I don't know about the years between that day under the tree and now, but I heard things."

"From who?"

"Don't forget, my dad and yours grew up together. They drifted apart after college, but every so often they'd touch base, catch up. Your dad was proud of you."

"I remember one time when just Dad and I visited Watertown. He took me to the police station and I met your dad, Officer Donovan. I was so excited, and probably drove him crazy with questions."

"Yeah? I guess I missed that. He would have loved it, though. He loves working in law enforcement. I was nervous when I had to tell him I was switching my major and going into the Forest Service. Policing the great outdoors instead of the streets of Watertown, or wherever I ended up after college. I started out to get a degree in Criminal Justice before I decided to change."

"Was he disappointed?"

Mike smiled. "If he was, he hid it well. But to be honest, I think all Dad wanted, Mom, too, was for me to succeed and be happy."

When she remained silent, Mike snaked his hand under the makeshift pillow barrier and poked her.

She jumped like a scared rabbit. "Hey, what was that for?"

"You're thinking too much again, but it's not about your

grandparents now, is it?"

The sadness that crept into her lovely eyes tore at him.

She fussed with the quilt, repositioned her pillow. "I couldn't be what Mom wanted. I tried. God knows I tried, but I failed." She sighed and turned her head toward him. "She wanted me to follow in Dad's footsteps. Having a daughter become a surgeon would have been a rather large feather in her societal hat."

"Instead you choose to treat patients who *had* feathers and keep them from becoming a decoration on anybody's hat. Fur too, for that matter."

Sam grinned, her eyes warmed. "You get it. I don't have to spell it out for you. I remember that day under the tree you sensed how I felt then too. That matters," she added, and slid her hand down to take hold of the one he'd used to poke her.

Then she yawned.

"Uh oh, guess talking worked. Darn, I was ready for plan B."

"I'm not quite there yet. Now you tell me something about you." Her eyes drooped. "One thing I remember. Once when I was just hitting my teens we came to town. I saw you... someplace, not sure where now, but you were with that weird buddy of yours."

"Al Murray. That weird buddy was my best pal growing up. Now he's my brother-in-law, but back then we were different, and took a lot of guff from the popular guys."

Now her eyes were closed, but a smile played across her relaxed features. "The so-called popular guys probably knew girls were crazy about you. You had that crooked little smile going for you and red hair."

"Oh, yeah, I worked on the Howdy Doody look."

"I wanted to go out with you so bad."

His head snapped around. "When? I don't remember you at that age. What were you twelve?"

"I was thirteen, you were sixteen. I saw you in Lil's store and almost wet my pants when you smiled at me. Lil told me maybe someday I'd fill out and you'd take me on a date. Who knew we'd end up in bed together?"

He waited. There had to be more than that, but her grip on his hand loosened and when he looked closer, he discovered she was breathing deeply, sound asleep.

Mike let go of her hand. He watched her as she slipped even deeper into sleep, but he couldn't quite settle. She'd filled out all right, and, they *were*, technically, in bed together.

Her confession kept running through his mind and with Samantha breathing softly beside him, it was well over an hour before *he'd* settled enough to sleep.

*****

The clock beside the bed read six a.m. Sam eased from under the covers, determined not to wake Mike. His back was to her, and only the top of his head was visible with all that rusty colored hair standing up in spikes. His beard matched the rusty red color, at least the *beginning* of a beard visible in the scruff on his jawline.

The man was indisputably sexy, which was why she tiptoed from the room before she caved in and ripped away that pillow barrier. She closed the bedroom door, visited the bathroom, and hunted up the clothes she'd left in her grandparents' room the night before. Once dressed, she pulled aside the heavy curtain at the window and opened the wooden shutters.

Her hopes sank. Snow fell in a white, fog-like curtain so that trees less than twenty feet from the cabin were hazy outlines. Their upper branches reached for the sky and disappeared in the thick falling snow, and the large evergreen behind the barn was a dark, triangular blur.

Once she'd made herself tea, Sam stood gazing out the front window. Tomorrow was Christmas Eve. Tears pushed against her eyelids. She leaned forward, squinting through the falling snow in the direction of her Pilot and Mike's truck. She figured they were well over fifty feet away, maybe more, and by now were no doubt well hidden beneath several feet of snow.

Could she use snowshoes and get to Mike's truck?

Did she dare try?

It would be lighter in about an hour and a half. Not much she could do before then except check on her moose. Then she'd roust her prince charming out of bed and see about fixing them some breakfast.

Al lifted his head when she entered the barn. Some of the food she'd left him was gone. Not as much as she'd liked, though. He did drink more offered water, keeping a wary eye on her as she held the bucket.

When she moved closer to check his leg, he reared his head back, never taking his eyes off her. "Easy, fella, I just want to see your leg."

There was a small amount of dried blood on the bandage. "Hmm, that's a good sign. No fresh bleeding." She decided it wasn't worth trying a closer examination and risking a sudden move. He was alert, drinking, and it appeared he'd at least taken a few bites of dried apple. He'd also been on his feet for a short time last night. Not a huge amount of progress, but not worse either.

She wrinkled her nose. The stall needed to be cleaned. "Later today you'll have to deal with me cleaning up in here, Al. I don't want to push it now, though, maybe later," she said, and left the stall.

Upon returning to the kitchen she was greeted by a rumpled, grumpy-looking, shirtless man. He rubbed the side of his face. "Guess I slept in. How long have you been up?"

She glanced at the clock on the wall. "A little over an hour. You were sleeping so soundly I didn't want to bother you. How do you feel?"

"Grubby, but otherwise not bad. My head isn't pounding like yesterday. I'm a little wobbly, but I think it's from not eating, not from a concussion. This is hunger, not nausea."

"That's a good sign. I checked and there's lots of breakfast stuff."

"I'd like to shower before we eat."

Sam gestured down the hall toward the bedrooms. "There should be towels in the closet next to the bathroom. Take your time."

She blew out a short breath as he walked away. His chest was covered with hair the same rusty color as the tangle on his head. She'd struggled to keep eye contact, and then shamelessly checked out his wide shoulders, broad back and tight behind as he walked away.

"Think breakfast," she muttered. "And Mike Donovan isn't on the menu. Darn it."

When Mike returned she was whipping up batter for pancakes and bacon sizzled in a pan. "Now I'm definitely feeling better. I love crisp bacon." He came up behind Sam and peered over her shoulder. A rich pine scent, one she recognized as the soap her grandpa stocked, engulfed her. "Are you making pancakes, Sam?"

"I am. Check the bacon, will you? If it's done, I'll get these started."

While they ate conversation was sparse, and mostly about the weather. The lake effect machine still churned, leaving little else to talk about for the time being.

Mike polished off three pancakes, refilled his coffee, and settled across from Sam. He pushed his chair back. "Thanks, Sam."

"You're welcome." Pouring hot water over a fresh tea bag, she studied him as she dunked the bag, then stirred and tapped her spoon on the cup. "You look much better, today. Not so pale. Any blurred vision, head pain? Does light bother you?"

"No blurred vision, and, now that you mention it, I didn't have to squint when I looked outside this morning." He held his hand out flat, tilted it back and forth. "As for my head, it hurts if I poke at it, but I removed the bandage and let water run over it in the shower without any bad reaction."

Sam nodded, leaned forward for a better look. "It looks good. I think a bandage is still a good idea. Something to keep it clean," she added.

Once she'd added milk and sweetener to her fresh tea, she folded her hands around her cup and leaned back. "You learned a lot about me last night. Now how about you? You're a federal wildlife officer. What made you take that road?"

Mike sipped, set his cup aside. "To become a federal wildlife officer, you have to like the outdoors because you'll be working in all kinds of weather." He grinned and nodded toward the window where snow fell thick and steady. "Case in point. I grew up in Watertown, and looked forward to the changing seasons. Sledding in winter, whitewater rafting in summer, I did it all. I have a special love for winter."

"Me too, usually," Sam admitted. "Not so much right now."

"Yeah, me neither, but see how light and fine that snow looks coming down? It's close to the powder they get out west." He appeared lost in thought as he stared at the window across the room. "Ever been sledding in Thompson Park?

"I love Thompson Park." A flood of memories filled Sam's head. "Grandpa taught me to cross country ski there."

"Huh, funny we didn't run into one another. I spent many a Saturday there, summer and winter. I worked at the zoo there one summer. Loved it. I think that's when I realized how much I like the outdoors and native animals."

"Hmmm, they have wolves. Are they considered native, then?"

"I think because we're so close to Canada and other areas where wolves are more common they consider them native to parts of New York State."

Sam rose to clear the table.

"Have you heard any howling since you've been up?" Mike gathered his plate and empty cup.

"No, and I checked on Al. He seemed... calmer, I guess, so maybe the wolf, or wolves, whichever, have moved on. Have you ever had to deal with wolves?"

"Not on the job. I've investigated sightings, one very recent, in fact, of wolves howling not far from here. So, a wolf passing through isn't out of the realm."

Sam ran water in the sink, added dish detergent. "Al lost a lot of blood. When I found him there was actually a pool in the snow."

"There was quite a bit at the accident scene, too. A hungry predator isn't going to ignore that tantalizing scent, especially during a blizzard."

While they cleared the table, Mike filled her in about the accident. As he slid his plate into the soapy water he asked, "Last night when we talked about career paths, did I mention Alan Murray and I went through training together once we'd switched paths?"

"Yeah, you did. I hope Al won't be offended by my naming a moose after him."

Mike laughed. "I doubt it. He'd probably get a kick out of it. As I mentioned, Al and I not only grew up together, we achieved two-year degrees in Criminal Justice together before switching. Wildlife officers are required to have at least that to apply. When done with training they're commissioned law enforcement officers, carry firearms and have to qualify every year just like police."

"Did it take a long time?"

49

"It felt like it at the time. After pre-land management training and orientation, I attended eighteen weeks of Land Management Police training at the Federal Law Enforcement Training Center -- FLETCO -- in Georgia. Then, three weeks at Federal Wildlife Officer -- FWOBE -- at a training center in Virginia, followed by ten weeks Field Training and Evaluation."

She'd stopped washing their dishes and gaped at him. "Really? I had no idea. I knew it was tough to get in, but had no idea what it took."

He leaned against the counter and crossed his arms. "Add an initial background investigation and psychological screening before entry. Then drug tests and periodical screening thereafter."

As they washed and dried the dishes Sam mulled over all Mike had just told her and, as she wiped down counters and put things away, an idea formed in her head.

"Would you cover me if I used snowshoes to get to your truck?"

Chapter Nine

Mike stopped, then placed a clean dish in the cupboard and slowly turned to face her. After a long moment, during which Sam kept those blue eyes intently focused on him, he folded the towel he'd been using and put it aside. "I'll give it some thought."

Sam's gaze never faltered as he left the room. He couldn't see her, he just *knew*.

He dug a sweatshirt from his duffle and pulled it on over his shirt. The hiss of water as he passed the bathroom alerted him she was in the shower, which bought him time to think about what he'd do next.

His knee jerk response was to trek through the snow himself and let *her* cover his ass. He felt better, almost normal, but concussions were nothing to fool with and symptoms could come back to bite you on that ass. Not a good scenario outside in the middle of a blizzard. Plus, he had no idea how skilled she was with a firearm. If someone was backing him up, he damn well wanted someone who knew what the hell they were doing.

Entering the stable, he closed the door behind him. First off, he stoked the woodstove to chase the chill, then crossed the room and rested his hands on the top rail of the stall. "Mornin', Al, how's it going?'

The moose swung his head around and looked up at Mike. He chewed slowly, kinda like a cow chewing its cud.

"Looks like dried apples, or whatever, were on your breakfast menu. I had pancakes, by the way." After a brief pause, Al went back to chewing. Mike chuckled. "I guess eating is a good sign, but I notice you're still not on your feet."

While Al continued to eat, Mike moved around inside the barn. He checked the outside door. It wasn't rattling in the wind like it had been the day before, but the latch wasn't as sturdy as he'd like it to be. Maybe he'd dig up some tools and see if he could tighten things up. The windows in the barn had inside shutters and were shut tight. He unlatched one and peeked out.

Snow still fell in silent, thick waves, but the flakes were coming straight down now, falling rather than being driven by wind.

He secured the shutter and went back to the stall. "The wind has died. That's a good sign, buddy."

The moose gave a rough kind of moaning growl. He lifted his ungainly head higher and stared at the door Mike had checked moments before. "What's the matter fella, you hear something?"

With each breath, Al emitted that moaning growl. His eyes were open wide.

Then Mike heard it, too. Scratching and thumping came from right outside the door. Out of habit his hand went to his side. "Damn," he muttered and tried to gage how long it would take to retrieve his gun from inside.

The door was solid. The latch worried him. He strode across the room toward the door leading into the house. He was reaching for the handle when it swung open and he staggered back. "Crap, Sam. Why don't you give a guy a warning?"

She brushed by him and hurried to Al's stall. "Did you hear that? I was in the hallway coming from the cabin and I heard something outside."

"I was just... let me see that," he demanded, pointing to the rifle she carried.

Al gave another of his coughing, moaning grunts.

Sam spun around, peering into the stall. "He's agitated, something has him spooked."

Mike strode over and took the rifle from her hands. "I heard something scratching at that door." He jerked his head in the direction of the outside door. "Actually, Al heard it before I did."

Sam rubbed her hands up and down her arms, shook her head. "I hope it holds. Grandpa planned to reinforce those doors."

Mike frowned at her.

"Bears," she said "We sometimes got bears wondering through. If he had a fawn or something being treated it guaranteed we'd all be safe."

Mike checked the rifle and made sure the safety was on, then gave a brisk nod. "A good reason, but I wish he'd followed up and fixed that latch. It's pretty crappy. More than half the bear population in New York State lives in the Adirondacks. Not all that far away, and they should be in hibernation now. If our visitor is a wolf, though, who's decided he'd like moose for dinner, we could have a problem if the latch fails."

"God, Mike. Wolves aren't aggressive."

"They aren't, normally. This guy may be sick or injured. Who knows? Wolves *are* curious, but as a rule avoid people."

Long minutes ticked by. Then Al gave one short low, growling moan and stretched his neck to nibble more dried fruit.

"It's gone. I'd bet on it." Sam glanced from her moose to Mike. "I want to look outside the door."

Mike slid a round into the Remington's chamber. "You crack the door open, not far, just enough to see outside. If I say shut it, don't ask why just shut the damn door."

Sam nodded and moved to release the latch. The shaky latch rattled and at first didn't budge. Using the heel of her hand, she shoved the lever holding it up and over. It clanked into place, and she held on to keep the door from flying open. "Ready?"

Mike lifted the rifle, aimed at the door and nodded.

Snow sifted through the widening crack as Sam eased the door open. When nothing filled the ever widening doorway, Mike lowered the gun and stepped forward.

He blew out a long breath, but when he breathed in again, it was like inhaling ice chips. "Damn, it's cold as a witch's--as witch's--"

"Hands?" offered Sam.

"At least." He ducked his head against the falling snow and leaned forward, glancing left and right. "He's gone, but there are tracks."

"Let me see." Sam squeezed into the open doorway beside him. "They're filling in fast, but they do look like wolf tracks."

Mike bent down and took a closer look. "There are scrape marks on the bottom of the door. They're fresh. Snow's banked against the back of the barn all along here, but not in front of the door."

He stood, nudged Sam back inside and closed the door. "It's a cliché, but I'd say we've had a wolf at the door. I want to find something to beef up this latch."

"Grandpa bought a new one last fall. I guess he didn't get it installed, but it's around her someplace."

"Okay." Looking around, Mike brushed off loose snow. He hunted around and found a length of heavy rope. "I'm going to rig this on the door until I get to the latch."

Sam helped him secure the door and after stoking the woodstove they lingered. Squatting in the stall, Sam smiled over her shoulder at Mike as she held the bucket and the moose drank long and deep. "This is good. He's had some food, and he's drinking." She rose and left the stall.

Leaning on the top rail, they both studied the prone moose.

"I have mixed feelings about him trying to stand."

Mike picked straw from her sleeve. "Why? Wouldn't it be a good thing for him to try and get up?"

"It's tricky. I don't want the leg to stiffen. It's not good for any large animal, horses, cows, or a full grown moose to lay down for any length of time. And remember, he may only be six or seven months old, but he already weighs as much as a pony or small horse."

"Okay, I get that. Plus, I suppose any struggle could open the wound and make it start bleeding again."

"So," Sam pushed away from the stall. "There's not much more we can do now but let him rest. You seemed comfortable handling Grandpa's rifle. Let's go inside and figure out what's the best way to retrieve your cell phone without getting attacked by a lone wolf."

Mike followed her back into the cabin. The woman had a one track mind. A headache lurked just behind his eyes, and this one he knew damn well wasn't from a concussion.

53

*****

Samantha paced, window to window, gaging the distance from the cabin's door to Mike's truck, or where she *thought* his truck was located.

"Would you quit pacing?" Mike dropped into a chair by the fireplace. He lifted a heavy iron utensil and poked at the simmering logs.

Sam gritted her teeth and swung around. How could he be so darned selfish? Didn't he care that her grandfather could be dying and... and what?

Her shoulders slumped. Mike had helped her lug an injured moose through a blizzard. He'd helped her treat the moose's wound, no questions asked. All after he'd put his life on the line coming after her through horrid conditions and had ended up getting a concussion to boot, for God's sake.

And here she was, acting as if her problems were all that mattered.

She stalked away, yanked open the refrigerator and pulled out a bottle of water, then studied Mike as he stirred the fire. He finished and leaned back in the overstuffed chair, stretching out his long legs.

A frown creased his brow and the fingers of his right hand drummed a steady beat on his denim clad thighs. She'd bet a hefty sum he was trying to figure out a way to help her without putting either of them in danger.

He was a tempting package, no argument. But in the past twenty four hours she'd discovered there was much more to her cabin mate than sexy green eyes and a buff body.

She twisted the lid from the water and took a sip. Mike was... solid, she decided, which was as good a term as any, along with determined, goal oriented, and loyal.

Unlike her situation with her mother, he'd not apologized when he'd switched to another field, another life goal, and not followed his father into law enforcement.

Actually, the situation was kind of funny. She'd switched from doctoring humans to doctoring animals; he'd switched from protecting towns and suburbs from two legged criminals, to protecting forests, lakes, streams *and* four legged creatures.

Well, *mostly* four-legged, along with owls, hawks, and eagles.

Her gaze drifted to the undecorated evergreen in the corner. Grandpa had placed it where Christmas Trees had been as far back as she remembered. A family tradition that had grounded her, giving her hope and courage when she'd needed it most.

"You look sad."

Sam jerked, almost dropping her water. Mike stood beside her, head tilted, those expressive eyes staring down at her.

"Sorry, I can't help it. I'm worried."

"About your Grandpa."

She shrugged and walked to the tree in the corner. Her fingers feathered over the springy branches, releasing the comforting scent of fresh pine. "I'm trying not to be maudlin."

She hated that her voice hitched and, as she stared at the empty tree branches, Mike placed his hands on her shoulders.

"Maudlin, now there's a word you don't hear every day."

She choked out a watery laugh, swiped at her cheek as a tear snuck out and slid down. "I'm sorry."

He gave her a little shake. "Stop apologizing. You're handling a hell of a lot. Bad timing all around."

His hands squeezed gently. They felt so warm, so... welcome, and exactly what she needed right then.

He released his grip when she turned and looked up at him. "You're a nice person, Mike. Here I am in a fix, and you show up being supportive despite your own problems."

He grinned. "Hey, at least this time we're not sitting under a tree."

"Ah, but there is a tree involved." Fighting tears, she turned to the naked tree. "Let's think positive. I'll get out the decorations later and you can help me decorate Grandpa's tree."

"My mom always let me do the lights, but she has her own style when it comes to the tinsel and other crap... or stuff," he amended. His eyes narrowed. "Are you going to be that strict, too?"

Her mood shifted and Sam laughed. "I am, so suck it up and do as you're told. In the meantime, though, we need to discuss how I'm going to strap on snowshoes and go get your cell out of your truck."

*****

He should have known she'd not give up so easily. Now *he* paced window to window, pausing at times to stare out, rubbing the back of his neck, considering. "I understand. But, damn it, Sam, there's a lot of risk involved. The storm has not let up. I'd say this one is a record breaker for lake effect."

"You'd know more about that than I would."

"You've spent enough time in Watertown during winter to know enough. Besides, have you forgotten about the wolf? Granted, it's very uncommon for wolves to attack people, but it's happened."

"I won't argue. There are usually certain circumstances, though."

"There hasn't been any rabies reported in wolves in this area recently. Raccoons, yeah, but for the most part, that's under control."

"I wasn't talking about rabies. I worked with a lot of people at the rehab center who'd dealt with wolves in captivity and in the wild. They're pack animals and have a strong pecking order."

Mike gingerly touched his bandaged head. "I'm aware of that. I also

55

know if they feel challenged it can provoke an attack."

"Again, circumstances prevail. I admit, they do have an extraordinary sense of smell, and--"

"And a bleeding animal, like maybe an injured moose, might draw in a hungry wolf. Agreed?"

She turned away, her back poker stiff as she walked to the window and stood in silence, peering out.

He hated arguing with her, hated being right. "Sam, you're a smart woman. Don't kid yourself or try to minimize the danger whoever goes out there will face."

When she turned around, it appeared all color had drained from her face. The scatter of freckles on her soft cheeks stood out like sprinkled cinnamon. The struggle raging inside her was evident in her incredible blue eyes.

"I hate asking you to help me do this." She closed her eyes and pressed her fingertips to them. When she dropped her hands and opened her eyes, Mike caved.

"I'll get your Grandpa's gun. The range is better than my handgun."

Her lip quivered. "Thank you," she whispered.

A short time later, he propped the loaded rifle against the wall by the door. Sam had donned several layers and pulled on sturdy boots. She appeared to use an ingrained checklist as she handled the snowshoes she'd retrieved from the barn.

"How's Al doing?" Mike asked, fascinated *and* impressed by her thorough inspection of each strap and buckle. He'd never gotten the knack of using snowshoes. Not from lack of trying, but cross-country skis were more his style and he could move along with the best of them.

She glanced up, her mind clearly elsewhere for a moment. "Oh, he looked good. He's still down, but all the food I put out is gone. I'll give him more when I get back."

He wasn't sure if it was confidence or stubbornness he detected, probably a little of both.

"Okay." Sam blew out a short breath. "Everything is in order. Do we have to go over this again?"

"You head straight to the truck, I cover your butt."

"Thank you, Mike. I--"

"If you thank me one more time I'm going to toss you out the door. Here's something for luck, though." He grasped her arms, yanked her close and lowered his lips to hers. He held tight, deepening the kiss, half expecting her to push him away and take a swing at him.

She didn't, so he slid his arms around her. In return, she wrapped *her* arms around him.

He softened the kiss, and as he started to pull away, she drew him back and pressed her lips to his again. Despite the layers she wore, soft curves pressed against him and his libido ricocheted like a round fired into a barrel.

He was about to scoop her up and forget about lost cell phones, snow storms and prowling wolves, when she broke away. Their lips were a breath apart, and her eyes gazed into his.

A slow smile curved her lips, still moist from that mind-blowing kiss. "I feel darned lucky."

Chapter Ten

Even wearing snowshoes, at times Samantha feared she'd never reach the small mountain of snow on the little rise ahead. The wind came in gusts, a change from yesterday's steady pounding, but still getting smacked in the face with occasional blasts of snow was like fighting her way face first through sharp needles.

She didn't dare look to either side, or heaven forbid behind her. If the wolf was stalking her, she'd know soon enough. One step at a time, keep focused on her goal and trust that Mike didn't lose sight of her.

She carried a light weight shovel they'd found in the garage. Mike had shortened the handle with a saw -- she hoped Grandpa would understand -- and it worked well as a walking stick as she slogged through snow. She didn't want to think about how much snow had accumulated since their arrival at the cabin, but a tight knot formed in her belly when she reached the snow mound, shoveled a couple of scoops of snow and looked down at the hood of Mike's truck.

She paused to catch her breath and look around. The cabin appeared hazy through the falling snow, and Mike's dark outline stood out in the doorway. "Stay there, Mike. Just stay there and pray I find that cell and make it back to you unscathed." She dug in and tossed aside the first shovelful of light, fluffy snow.

Determined, she continued one shovel at a time, fashioning a deep, wide crater beside the emerging truck. "Like shoveling powdered sugar," she muttered.

When she finally reached the truck's door, she was hip deep in snow. She enlarged the area, using the shovel and sometimes her body to create a space big enough to get the door open. All she needed was enough room to slip her arm inside and reach the phone. If it was where he said he'd tossed it.

Satisfied at last, she stuck the shovel in the snow. Pawing the sifting white aside she managed to tug the door open. Snow poured in, covering the front passenger seat.

"Great, Mike will be thrilled. Now where..." She removed one glove and carefully felt around with her hand. By the time her searching fingers closed over the familiar shape, they were numb.

Shoving the phone into her pocket, she zipped it closed and pulled her glove on. Her hand stung, burning like fire from exposure. She climbed from the truck and it was like climbing from a dim, snow encased cave. Once outside she plopped down in the snow, taking a moment to rest before tackling the rest of the climb from the hole she'd fashioned to reach the door. While she rested, she cleared her head, bringing the memory of the pathway she'd created to get there into her mind's eye.

She rose and searched the spot where she'd stuck the shovel. It had tipped over, and she had to dig for it. "Of course," she muttered, tossing snow left and right. "If I didn't need it, I'd leave the darned thing here."

Then her hand closed on the shortened handle. She straightened, and froze in place. Her grip tightened like a vice on the shovel's handle.

Less than a dozen feet away blocking the pathway stood the wolf. He lowered his head, his yellow-eyed, unwavering gaze fixed on her. Seconds passed like dripping syrup, but her mind raced.

If she looked away the move could translate as submission or fear. If she didn't, a challenge.

Crap.

She took slow even breaths, sorting details. This was no healthy wolf. His coat was patchy, his sides sunken. From her vantage point it was hard to tell, but she gaged him at a hundred and twenty pounds, give or take. "Okay, big guy, I'm standing my ground. I'm not your dinner. See, no antlers, no fur."

Her voice sounded shaky and weak, not good. She swallowed several times to dispel the lump lodged in her throat. Slowly she shifted the shovel in front of her, gripping the handle with both hands.

The wolf's head lowered even more.

She raised the shovel horizontally, like a barrier.

"I'm not backing down, big guy." Her voice came out stronger this time. "So make up your mind. Fight or flight."

*****

Mike sucked in a sharp breath. Like a misty shadow, the wolf had stepped onto the pathway. Seconds later, Sam's head and shoulders rose above the snow pit she'd created.

Had the wolf been there all along, watching, waiting?

Mike's heart thudded, ringing in his ears. He moved forward and flipped off the rifle's safety. The air was bone chilling cold, but sweat dampened his palms.

The wolf blocked the pathway. If he fired and missed he could hit Sam. On the plus side the wind was coming at him, and so far the wolf wasn't aware of him. He wasn't wearing snowshoes and sunk in above his knees as he waded forward.

Sam kept the shovel in front of her. Smart girl. She squared her shoulders and her lips moved, but the wind swallowed her words.

The wolf lowered his head.

"Hey!" Mike yelled as loud as he could, closing the distance,

59

struggling to push his way through the near impenetrable white wall. The wolf's ears swiveled, but he kept his focus on Sam.

Mike called out again.

"Hey!" Sam's faint response echoed his cry. Thank, God this time she'd heard him. He moved closer until he was about fifteen feet behind the wolf. Bracing against the buffeting wind, he raised the rifle.

"Go, get out!" This time Sam's voice rang clearer.

"You heard her, you mangy beast!" he yelled, and the wolf jerked sideways, swinging his head around. "Yeah, you son-of-a bitch, I've got you in my sights. Sam," he called out. "Can you hear me?"

"I hear you."

The wolf crouched sideways on the path, his head swung left to right, his sinister gaze moving from Sam to Mike, then back to Sam.

"I'm going to count to three, out loud. On three I want you to drop."

He sensed, rather than saw her hesitation. "Don't second guess him, Sam. He can be on you in seconds. I don't have a choice. Ready?"

She nodded and lowered the shovel.

"One, two," he shouted, then sucked in a deep breath, took aim and...

The wolf left the path, wading into the deep snow, plowing his way through. He appeared to stagger, but he made it to the tree line and within seconds faded into the forest like a silent gray ghost.

Mike lowered the rifle and nearly lost his footing when Sam plowed into him and wrapped her arms around him.

He pried her arms loose. "You're okay. You're okay," He repeated. "Let's get the hell inside."

They fought their way back and stumbled through the door into warmth and safety.

Mike propped the rifle against the wall and began to shed his outdoor gear. The adrenalin crash would come, but at the moment he felt charged, energized, ready for anything. Smiling as he bent to remove his boots. "Wow, I can't believe that sucker backed down like that. That was one big-assed, mangy wolf,"

He straightened, and his smile faded.

Sam hadn't moved since she'd burst through the door beside him. Her arms hung limp at her sides, melting snow pooled at her feet. Her face was paper white and she shook, visibly, from head to toe.

Mike stepped to her. Her eyes lifted and met his gaze, locking there, unblinking as he began to loosen her gear.

"It's okay, we're safe." He pulled off her gloves, tossed them aside and unzipped her coat. "Maybe we'll open some of that exceptional wine in your grandparents' pantry. I sure could use a nice glass of Merlot."

After he'd undone the snowshoes and stripped off the outer layers, he led her to the fireplace, made her sit, and knelt to remove her boots.

He remained on his knees, eye level with Sam, and took her hands in his. They were shaking, and stone cold.

Her voice cracked. "Would you hold me, Mike? Please, just hold me." She came into his arms like a frightened child, wrapping her arms around his neck. He eased onto the sofa, loosened the death grip on his neck and lodged himself into the corner.

He settled her against him. She was frightened all right, but this was no child pressed against him. This was a woman, and he feared with the trauma of facing the wolf, the unknown status of her grandfather and their situation in general, she'd emotionally hit the wall.

He'd treated shock. Hauled injured colleagues from raging streams and cornered armed poachers.

He'd held women before, too, but this wasn't just any woman. This wasn't a chance meeting that clicked for two healthy adults headed down that 'mutual consent' path. Oh, no. This was Samantha, the kid from his past.

Only she wasn't a kid anymore.

*****

Sam burrowed in, hiding her face against Mike's shoulder. He murmured soft, indistinguishable words and in a strange way reminded her of that day under the tree when he'd come to her.

He held her, giving her the comfort she needed as emptiness spread inside her. This situation was too much to face alone. And thank God she didn't have to.

She lifted her head, gazed into his eyes. There was strength in them, yet gentleness. "Don't let go yet, Mike."

His arms tightened. "No problem."

Gradually the uncontrollable shaking eased. She tried to settle, burrowing closer and closing her eyes. "He was in bad shape, Mike. Very thin and I think there was blood on his coat. This time of year his coat should have been in prime condition."

Mike skimmed his hand up and down her back, comforting. "His wasn't. I'd say he's a loner, too."

"I agree," Sam said, and relaxed a little more against Mike. "He's more than likely been driven from the pack. It usually happens to young adult males. His condition made it hard to determine his age, and it wasn't my first priority. He may have been howling to seek other wolves, but if he was unable to be part of a pack, to contribute due to injury or illness, the pack would turn on him and kill him."

Mike's heart beat slow and steady beneath her head resting on his chest. Going over everything, putting the incident into perspective and behind her helped. Her eyes grew heavy, her pulse steadied.

She shifted, slipping her arms around his neck and pressing her face

61

to his beard-roughened cheek. His skin radiated heat. She pressed her body closer, and the warmth spread throughout her body.

He turned his head and her lips brushed the corner of his mouth. "Sam," he murmured, his breath warm on her face, "I think maybe we should--"

He went still when she pressed her lips to his and cut him off.

She combed her fingers into his hair, pulling him in, sealing the kiss. Mike slid his hands down and grasped her waist. When she broke the kiss, he blew out a long breath and eased her away.

"God, Sam. I'm no saint. If you keep going..." He shook his head. "No, Sam, not like this."

Moments ticked by in silence. In the fireplace, hot coals simmered and hissed.

She studied his rugged face. Deep lines creased his brow, and his wary eyes, darkened to a deep, forest green, revealed nothing. "I need to shut down my mind, Mike, to lose myself and just *feel*," she whispered.

With a strangled moan, he pulled her in and closed his mouth over hers. Seconds later, he broke away. "Hang on," he said. Breathing hard he maneuvered her across his body, gathered her into his arms and rose.

He crossed the room in long strides. She pressed her face into the warm curve of his neck and held on. The darkened bedroom was cool and she clung to him, not wanting to lose the warmth emanating from him. He placed her gently on the bed and straightened. Confused, she gazed up at him.

"I'm going to regret saying this the minute it comes out of my mouth." He dragged his hand over his face. "We need to stop and take a step back."

She closed her eyes and lay very still.

He tugged the heavy quilt from beneath her and tucked it around her. Embarrassed, her cheeks burned and she turned her head away.

What had she done?

His rejection was a clear message that he regarded her blatant come on as another empty-headed move by a woman with no more sense than a brick.

"Sam, look at me."

She refused, and closing her eyes muttered, "Go away. I don't know what I was thinking."

"You don't know what I'm thinking either, damn it. Look at me."

When she did, his eyes fixed on hers and her heart lurched.

"Don't for one damn minute think I don't want you." He reached down and brushed a tangled strand of hair from her face. "The timing's wrong. We've had one hell of a day. A couple of them," he added. "I'll not hold you to your offer." Blood rushed to her face and he grinned. "But I could be persuaded to reconsider when we've both rested and adrenalin mixed with hormones isn't running the show."

Sam tugged the quilt tighter beneath her chin. "I see what they meant about your charm."

"Who are they?"

"Girls, Mike, the ones you thought were teasing you when all they wanted was to get their hooks in you."

His obvious confusion made her smile and tension gripping her neck and shoulders eased. He didn't have a clue what she meant. Gentleman to the end, he'd resisted her, all part of his charm.

But, he'd left the door open. Charming as a kitten, or wily like a fox?

He leaned down and kissed her. "Get some rest. I'm going to do the same." He started to back away, then paused. "My cell, did you get it?"

How in God's name had she forgotten? "It's in my coat pocket, the one with a zipper on the right hand side," she said, and started to push the quilt aside.

He stopped her. "I'll find it."

"I want to call my grandparents."

She attempted to rise, and he placed both hands on her shoulders. "Stop, Sam. The phone's probably dead. I had it on when I followed you, but when I ditched the truck I don't remember if I turned it off."

"You have a charger, right?"

He straightened and scratched his head. "Yeah, there's one in the truck. And no, we're not going back out there. Not now. If the phone's dead, we can't risk using the charger and draining the truck's battery."

She frowned up at him. He was right. Much as she wanted to spring out of bed, her thoughts were sluggish, her arms and legs weighed like wet cement and her eyes were losing their focus. "I guess you're right," she murmured. "I can't think now."

Drifting, she closed her eyes. "I'll take a nap," she murmured.

The door closed with a soft click, leaving Sam alone.

*****

Mike located Sam's jacket and found his cell. A quick check confirmed what he'd feared and he clicked it off. His battery barely registered, and their remote location coupled with the lousy weather was bound to be an issue.

He knelt and fed the fire. When the flames danced and crackled, he grabbed a throw and settled on the couch. He was an idiot, he decided as he punched a pretty red pillow into shape and flopped onto his side facing the fire.

If he wasn't so damn... such a damn... *gentleman,* he'd be snuggled up with a willing woman right now instead of laying on a lumpy sofa by himself. But then what? When she realized what she'd done she'd hate his guts for taking advantage of the situation.

After a trauma, or a life threatening experience the need to connect with another human was normal. That need, or want, took many forms. Near the top of the list was sex. He'd studied human behavior in college and that closeness, that reaffirmation of life was strong.

Who was he kidding? His pulse went wild and his brain went fuzzy when he'd had Samantha Gates in his arms, and neither response had anything to do with reaffirming life.

Bending his knees to accommodate his makeshift bed, he readjusted and resettled. A headache lingered just behind his eyes. He glanced at the mantle clock and tried to ignore nagging pangs of hunger. How could it be afternoon? He dragged the heavy throw higher, leaving only his nose and eyes exposed. There'd been no sound from behind the bedroom door since he'd left Sam. A couple hours of rest would do them both good.

While the dancing fire relaxed his body, his mind drifted.

Tomorrow was Christmas Eve. His parents were no doubt worried about him, and when, *if*, they reached someone with his cell before it died he'd make sure they were notified.

Traditions created over the years and carried out every Christmas for as far back as he remembered were good ones, simple, but good. Aunts, uncles and whatever cousins were in town stopped by before church. Al and his sister Janie usually came by, too.

Probably not this year, though. Through a sleepy smile he pictured his best friend since childhood as a new dad, his sister a mom. They'd be good parents. As soon as he got out of this mess he'd buy the newest Murray the biggest teddy bear he could find.

As sleep took him under, his head filled with dreams of Christmases past and of Samantha Gates running to him through softly falling snow.

Chapter Eleven

Sam jerked awake. Disoriented, she gazed around. Outside the window soft twilight signaled approaching darkness.

She pushed up and shoved aside her disheveled hair. Swinging her feet to the floor she stood and, with her arms wrapped around her for warmth, she hunched her shoulders and moved to the window.

Still snowing. Never in all the times she'd visited Watertown in winter had a lake effect storm lasted this long. Grandpa had told her about such storms, but she'd thought he was exaggerating.

"Guess you weren't kidding, Grandpa."

On her way to the bathroom she noticed the cabin was quiet, not a sound came from down the hall. No movement, no smell of fresh brewed coffee.

She splashed water on her face and combed her hair. Peering into the mirror, she studied her face. Clear blue eyes, average skin. Except for the freckles scattered across the bridge of her nose the image reflected back at her wasn't bad.

Her cheeks flushed. What had gotten into her? She'd thrown herself at Mike, crawled all over him. How could she face him now?

The light was almost gone when she stepped into the main room. And there he was, sound asleep with only the top of his head poking out from beneath Grandma's throw. The fire had died to simmering coals and there was a chill in the room.

Sam glanced around. Where was the cell phone? Had he found it, did he try it? Part of her wanted to shake him awake and demand the answer, and part of her wanted to crawl beneath that throw, snuggle in and wake him with a kiss.

The desire to snuggle alerted her that whatever had possessed her earlier still had its claws dug in. The best thing she could do right now was to go check on her moose and keep busy until all those absurd urges dissipated.

The barn was cold and dark. She realized with all the excitement they'd forgotten to leave a light on, and she made her way carefully to the woodstove. Moments later, the wood she'd fed into the ancient stove caught and she paused, warming her hands.

She went still at the sound of movement from the stall across the room. "Al, are you all right?" Flipping on the overhead light, she gasped when she spotted Al's huge head resting on the top rail of the stall.

"Oh, oh my God." She hurried across the room. He'd been up before, but this time he looked more alert, almost normal. He lifted his head and gave one of his grunting coughs.

Tears sprung to Sam's eyes. She held her hand out and stroked his nose, edging closer to get a look at his injured leg.

The bandage had loosened, but there was no sign of fresh bleeding. With wary eyes he studied her as she opened the door to the stall. "I'm not going to hurt you," she said, keeping her voice steady. "Don't get it into your head to hurt me, okay?"

She moved closer. When he showed no sign of panic or aggression she touched him, running a gentle hand down his neck. "I bet you're hungry and thirsty, huh, fella."

He grunted, sidestepping a little.

Sam backed away and left the stall. She returned with water and a large container of dried fruit and vegetables. "Sorry, Grandma," she muttered as she knelt and broke carrots into smaller pieces. "I'll get to the store as soon as I can and stock up your winter pantry. Here you go." She slid the bucket of water closer to the moose, who'd been eyeing her offering with interest.

She barely had time to place the water in front of him and dump the dried apples and carrots before he lowered his head and began to eat. With his attention devoted to his late day meal, she was able to get a close look at his leg.

The bandage came off with little effort. Sam winced at the raw gash and tiny jagged cuts that ran from shoulder to knee. Her concern now was the danger of infection. Somehow she had to treat and rewrap the wound.

Al munched away, paying no attention. He paused long enough to drink, and then lifted his head. He sniffed his injury, and then shifted his attention to Sam as she replenished his food and gathered supplies. She doubted he'd tolerate heavy cleansing of the wound, but there were antiseptic wipes available and they'd be better than nothing.

He was a good patient, and a wide grin split her face when she finished treating and wrapping his leg with only a few fidgets and grunts from the moose.

She gathered her supplies and, stepping from the stall, almost laughed out loud when he circled the stall. He limped, but her moose was on the mend.

The door to the barn opened and Sam swung around. Her happiness bubbled over and she couldn't stop grinning. "Hey, sleepy head, look at our moose."

Mike crossed to the stall. As if on cue, Al once more circled the stall.

"He's showing off for you." Sam elbowed Mike, and he turned, gazing down at her.

His sleepy-eyed gaze met hers, locked on and held. "Yeah?"

Sam's knees went soft. In her excitement she'd forgotten what had occurred between them. Flustered, she broke eye contact and nodded toward the shuffling moose. "He was on his feet when I came in and even let me treat his leg and apply a new dressing. He's limping, but he's moving." She was rambling, but welcomed the distraction. "And look, look at him eat."

Al ignored his visitors and munched down apples.

Mike leaned on the top rail, frowning as he looked into the stall. "You went in there yourself?"

"He was okay, I--"

"With a five hundred pound injured moose." He turned, crossed his arms and stared at her.

Sam's upbeat mood plunged. Once again he'd made it clear he questioned her judgement. Weak knees forgotten, her spine stiffened. "I assessed the situation, Mike, and I resent you treating me as if I'm incapable of making smart decisions."

"Oh, right, like driving off into a friggin' snowstorm to a remote cabin?"

She slammed drawers and doors, stashing the medical supplies. How could she be attracted to a man who still thought of her as an empty headed child?

"I stoked the wood burner," she said, jerking her head toward the stove. "Without burning my fingers, how about that? I don't know about you, but I'm starving and I need to try and call my grandparents." She wiped off the counter and tossed a paper towel in the trash. "Did you find your cell?

"Yeah, I found it."

His tone and expression made her hopes plunge. She bit her lip, fighting back unwelcome tears. Why did these confrontations leave her emotional and weak? "Good. I'll dig up some food. You get that damn cell phone and make it *work!*"

Embarrassed by the hitch in her voice, Sam slammed the door behind her. She paused, pressing her hands to her eyes. Once under control, she continued on to the kitchen. She'd lost her appetite, but fixing something to eat would keep her occupied and maybe, just maybe keep her from taking a swing at his smug, handsome face.

*****

Mike winced when the door slammed. "Well, I handled that well," he muttered, glancing over his shoulder when Al nudged him. "You're responsible, you know." He reached out a tentative hand and rubbed the soft, ugly nose with his knuckles. "You're supposed to be a wild animal. You should have threatened her, stomped your feet. Or something," he added, breaking into a smile as the ungainly beast nudged him again as if to say 'don't stop rubbing my nose, it feels good.'

The moose's progress was good news. The expression on Sam's face when he'd entered the barn had reflected her excitement. "Shit, Al, I kind of squashed her mood, didn't I? I overreacted, and I hurt her."

Al went back to munching his dried goodies.

"Sure, ignore me. You're the only guy I can unload on and all you can think about is feeding your face. I behaved like an idiot. Again. Earlier, I turned down an opportunity most guys would dive into without a second thought. But no, I had to be noble, damn it, and now I've hit the other end of the spectrum. I'm either a gentleman, or an insensitive jerk. There's got to be a middle ground, but because I've never been here before the ground is damn shaky."

He shook his head. "And now I'm unloading my crazed state of mind on a moose."

With a grunt that could have been interpreted as agreement, Al circled, pawed at the straw, and then folded his legs, lowering to the floor. He nosed the new bandage and repositioned the injured leg.

Mike dragged his feet. Apologizing for being a jerk didn't appeal, but the gentleman would settle for nothing less. He heaved a sign and opened the door to the cabin.

She had her back to him and something sizzled in a pan on the stove. With quick, firm cuts she chopped greens with a rather big knife. When he closed the door behind him, she glanced over, tossed down the knife -- a move he appreciated given her current mood -- and swung around, facing him. "Where's the phone?"

"I'll get it," he said, and crossed the room. This wasn't a good time to get into feelings and apologies. Too complicated. She wasn't about to detour from her goal, and he couldn't blame her. He only hoped if they managed to reach someone in Watertown the news would be good.

She turned down the heat under the sizzling pan and followed him.

He picked up his cell and waited until she joined him. "I checked it earlier and it was hovering at about ten percent, so I turned it off."

Sam wiped her hands on a towel tucked into her waistband. "How about reception?"

He shook his head. "I didn't take the time. Sam." He touched her arm. She stiffened, glanced down at his hand.

"Get it over with, Mike. I'm not going to freak out if we can't make a call. Just turn the darned thing on and let's find out."

He pressed the tab on the side of his phone and watched it cycle through opening. When the screen lit, he checked the towers. "Crap," he muttered when it flipped from one to two, then back to one. "Not good."

"Who shall we call?" She rubbed one hand up and down her arm.

"I have my mom and dad on speed dial. They're the closest."

He held his breath and pressed the key. The ringing broke up, as if not going through. He frowned and Sam's shoulders slumped.

Then suddenly a familiar voice shouted in his ear. "Mike, son, where are you?"

"Dad, listen. I don't have much power. I'm with Samantha at the Gates cabin. We're fine."

"Thank, God. Your mother--"

"Dad, how is Charley Gates?"

The line cut out, crackled and his father's voice faded.

"What? What did you say?" Mike shouted, although it wouldn't make a damn bit of difference if the connection was dropped.

Like magic, his dad's voice cut in again. "Charley is okay, he's--"

This time when the line went dead the screen went black.

Sam gripped his arm and he closed his hand over her trembling fingers. Tears glistened in her eyes.

"Sam, don't," he began, but she gave her head a firm shake.

"Mike," she spoke softly. "These aren't sad tears, they're pure relief. He's alive." She squeezed his arm. "It's enough for now."

She released her grip and returned to the stove. Mike stared at her, stared at the dead phone in his hand.

"I have to believe he'll be all right, Mike," she said, as she readjusted the heat. "We'll eat, and then trim the tree."

His gaze landed on the bare tree across the room. He admired her strength and welcomed her optimism. "I get to do the lights, right?"

She chuckled. "Yeah, and then maybe I'll let you help me do the rest. Now go wash up and comb your hair. You look like a vagrant."

*****

Sam dived into making a batch of Sloppy Joe sandwiches. Anything to keep busy and the simple task kept her mind from wondering and her imagination from exploding out of hand.

Grandpa was alive. For now she'd cling to that one simple truth. He was strong, healthy and in the prime of his life. He'd never been sick, at least that she remembered.

The Manwich sauce sizzled as she coated the ground beef. A few feet away Mike frowned at the apple she'd instructed him to slice. He'd voiced a preference for fries, a strong preference, and the sullen way he chopped the crisp Red Delicious apples clearly reflected his disappointment.

He looked up when she tapped the spoon on the skillet. "I'll do some baking later," she said. "Will that make up for no fries?"

Mike popped a slice of apple into his mouth. "It'll help. What else are we having with our SJ's?"

"I checked supplies and tossed together a spinach salad while you were cleaning up. You do like spinach, don't you?"

He shrugged, crunched another bite of apple. "Not a favorite."

69

"I think you'll like my version. Grandma gave me this one."

"I guess I'm willing to reconsider and give it a try."

Mike went back to slicing, and Sam gathered ingredients to make her grandmother's dressing, thankful they were avoiding what had happened earlier. Thoughts of her grandparents crowded her mind right now. Anything else would add even more emotional upheaval.

She'd memorized the recipe for Grandma's dressing and while she combined the ingredients, couldn't help but wonder what her grandma was doing now. How was she coping? How was Grandpa? The brief comment from Mike's dad gave her hope, but she knew there could be more to deal with once the storm ended.

She got out plates for their sandwiches, gave the meat another stir. Dressed salads were put in the fridge to chill. Pausing, she gazed out the window. Mesmerized by the falling snow, she heaved a deep sigh. The rolling, white landscape was a stark shot of reality.

"Hey, your mood's slipping." Mike came up behind her and placed his hands on her shoulders. "We're going to get through this, Sam. Hang on to the good stuff, the good news."

Sam closed her eyes. She'd tried hard to hide the doubts churning inside her, but sensed Mike saw right through her attempt. "I'm glad you're here," she murmured. "And I'm sorry I've been such a pain."

His hands tightened on her shoulders. "And I've been such a pleasant soul?" He turned her to face him. "I've learned a lot about you in a short time, Sam, and I'll admit to several misconceptions."

Her pulse skittered and jumped when she opened her eyes. They stood face to face, his hands still warm on her shoulders. She wasn't sure what he meant. Did he like her, or was she even worse than he'd imagined?

As she gazed into focused green eyes, he gave a considering, "Hmmm," and then leaned in and kissed her.

Her heart slammed against her ribs.

The unforeseen kiss startled her. Too stunned to react, Sam did nothing until Mike ended the kiss.

"Well, now I'm wondering about those misconceptions." She rubbed her lips together. "Are you reconsidering me, kinda like the spinach?"

She took a step back.

He pulled her in for another kiss, one not quite so hesitant or gentle. This time he drew her closer and her body pressed against him.

When the kiss ended she took a deep breath. "I guess that wasn't about spinach."

Mike laughed out loud and she stepped back, forcing him to release his physical hold on her. His unwavering gaze held her prisoner a bit longer. Once her racing heart settled she huffed out a short breath. "You get the salads. I'll raid Grandpa's wine supply."

Mike nodded slowly. "Okay."

"Red should go with Sloppy Joes, right?"

"Yeah," Mike said. "Red works for me."

He went to retrieve the salads, and Sam went for a nice Merlot.

Chapter Twelve

Their relationship had shifted. A big change, monumental, Mike determined as they forked up chilled salads. Since they'd started eating, there'd been declining conversation. In an effort to lighten the mood, Mike poked at his salad. "What are these little red things?" He'd decided spinach wasn't so bad and kept that info to himself, but couldn't resist poking Sam like he'd poked the salad.

"They're pomegranate seeds."

"Why just use the seeds? Why not chucks of pomegranate?"

"Are you always this difficult when trying new things, or is this just for my benefit?"

He couldn't resist a grin. "I like to know more about the unknown before I try it."

Sam opened her mouth, then closed it and reached for her wine. After a slow, careful sip, she set her glass aside and touched a napkin to her lips. "I take it we aren't talking about pomegranates any more than we were about spinach earlier."

She picked up the bottle of Merlot and topped off his glass. Mike's brow lifted when she topped hers off too. "Misconceptions," she began, leaning back and swirling the wine in her glass. "Would you care to share what you meant when you said you'd had misconceptions about me?"

Mike suspected the wine supplied the courage for her pointed question. This was her third glass. He rested his elbows on the table. "Umm, I hadn't given you much thought prior to yesterday. The most vivid memory I had was the one from when we were kids that time under the tree."

"Was it a good one?"

"Very," he said, and took a sip of wine. "The rest are vague. That day under the tree stood out."

"Why?"

He swirled his wine, stared into the crimson depths. "I was scared to death my dog was going to die and without even knowing me you reached out and did the right thing."

"Yesterday you called me reckless and accused me of taking off into a snowstorm without thinking."

"I did, but it was in the heat of the moment, or in this case, a damn cold moment."

That teased a smile out of her.

"Let me ask you this, Sam. Why do you feel you have to apologize for going after what you want?"

Sam sipped, lowered her glass and lifted her gaze to meet his. "You'll see through anything I try to evade, won't you?"

"I possess a well-developed bullshit detector."

"From being raised by a cop?"

"Could be, but this isn't about me. Let's not shift direction. You've obviously worked hard to get where you are today. It shows," he added.

"Have you reached that conclusion because even though I sometimes appear to ignore common sense, other times I actually know what I'm doing, like patching up an injured moose?"

Mike tilted his head and studied her. Learning what had occurred from the time he met a stubborn little girl under a tree till now had all of a sudden become important. "Let's just say patching up a five hundred pound moose without flinching not only surprised me, it stirred my interest in you."

"The interest is mutual, by the way," Sam said, and then tilted her head, studying him right back. "Here's a brief synopsis of the life and times of Samantha Gates. At least up to this point, and," she added, "in return, will I get quid pro quo from Michael Donovan?"

"Rather boring, but, yeah, I can do that."

Sam took a healthy sip of wine, rose and began to clear their dishes. "Revealing my life and times will be less stressful if I keep busy."

"Sam, this isn't an interrogation."

She paused and laid her hand on his shoulder. "I know, Mike. Just let me work this through the best way I know how."

He touched her hand. The connection was brief, yet his stomach muscles tightened. He had to know more, to know *all*, about this intriguing woman.

She lifted her hand and moved away. "The first time we met I was having a full blown tantrum."

"You were upset with your parents."

"An understatement, but I settled when I got my way. Grandpa made them promise to let me spend the holidays in Watertown with them." She paused to rinse their plates and turned, facing him as she wiped her hands. "At the time, I figured I'd won the battle. It wasn't until a couple years later that I realized it hadn't been much of a battle at all. Mom was relieved when she didn't have to deal with making her daughter fit in with the biggest social events of the year."

Sadness darkened her pretty eyes and made Mike want to stop her right there and gather her into his arms. She looked defeated, but she also looked determined, and he recognized the need for her to finish.

"During the Christmas season Dad's position demanded a lot of social interaction. Mom loved her role. Don't get me wrong, my mom was, and still is, a perfect prominent surgeon's wife."

73

Nancy Kay

"Your mom's a beautiful woman. You're different, Sam. You're beautiful, too, but in a different way."

"You're a nice man, Mike."

"No, I mean it. I'm not sucking up to you to make you feel good. When your mom was a teenager I'll bet her goals were different from yours, a lot different," he emphasized.

"You're right. She was prom queen and in tune with the latest trends in clothes and makeup. On the contrary, I drove her nuts. No matter how many times she dragged me to the salon, I'd yank my hair back into a tail and go traipsing off into the woods. I also refused to use the stuff she bought me to hide my freckles."

"I like your freckles," Mike declared, grinning at her.

She responded with a lopsided smile. "I wanted to try that junk so bad. I hated having freckles back then, but refused to do what my mother wanted just on principle." She pointed to her nose. "I still have them, and I've become vain enough to use make up now and then. We fought about clothes a lot, too." Sam's face turned slightly pink beneath her freckles. "She had to give up dressing me like a fashion model when I had the audacity to develop a chest."

Mike struggled. It pained him to keep his gaze fixed on her face. However, he briefly and shamelessly indulged in a brief fantasy about where else on her body he might find freckles.

Folding the cloth she'd used to wipe the counters, Sam picked up her wine and peered into the almost empty glass. "Hmm, how much Merlot did I consume? Because I think I've given you way too much information. So," she continued, after tipping her glass and draining it. "To shorten this long boring story, I was lucky to have grandparents who understood me. I suspect Dad did too, a lot more than he let on in front of my mother. He never disagreed with her, but he maneuvered around the obvious while letting me know that even though my dreams weren't what Mom wanted for me, he understood. Dad urged me to follow my heart."

She gave a quick, decisive nod. "So I did. And here I am." She shifted her gaze to Mike. "I'm well on my way to being a vet, like Grandpa. There'll always be a nagging sense that I let my mother down." She shrugged. "I deal with it."

"Your grandfather must be very proud of you."

"And that helps me deal."

Mike rose and, taking the empty glass from her, he set it aside. He took her hands in his. "My first impression was formed that day in a snow storm under a tree. Brat came to mind, but softened when you put your own problems aside to comfort me as I dealt with mine."

She bit her lip, raising her gaze to meet his. "And once again you've come after me during a snow storm. This time risking your life and probably screwing up your Christmas with your family."

74

He kissed her forehead. "My family will be there when the snow stops. As for Christmas, it appears we've got all the makings at our fingertips, thanks to your grandpa. I *do* get to do the lights, right?"

"That's right. I'll get the boxes from storage, you finish up here. Then while you get started on the tree, I'll get started on cookies."

Before she could walk away, he lifted his hand and ran his finger over the bridge of her nose.

For a long moment they gazed at one another. Then Sam stretched up and touched her lips to his. "Thanks for listening," she murmured.

Mike released her hand and stared after her as she hurried away. "Any time, Sam," he said softly.

*****

Humming along with classic holiday tunes, Sam folded whipped butter into dry ingredients. She glanced over where Mike draped tiny white lights amongst thick evergreen branches. "Make sure you don't put them all to the outside. Tuck them *into* the branches."

"Yeah, yeah, you've mentioned that a couple hundred times." He shot her a fast grin. "I don't smell anything baking yet."

"Baking from scratch takes time. I don't just slice logs of dough and pop them into the oven."

"Don't knock Pillsbury chocolate chippers. They're easy and convenient."

Sam widened her eyes in mock horror. "Tell me you don't actually make those," she said, scooping measured portions of lemon cookie dough onto a baking sheet.

He stood back, eyeing his work. "Doughboy is my friend, especially when I'm short on time and need to impress a... ah, guest."

Sam slid the cookies into the heated oven and closed the door. "Is guest code for date?"

"Guest, date, whatever." Mike strolled over, eyed the empty mixing bowl and sniffed. "Umm, smells lemony. When will they be done?"

Sam set the oven timer then grabbed the empty bowl and took it to the sink. "Twelve minutes, and for the record, if I was the *date* you were trying to impress, you'd lose points with those fake cookies. Speaking of your love life, while those cookies bake and I stir up another batch, why don't you give me that quid pro quo about the life and times of Michael Donovan?"

He retrieved a bottle of water from the fridge, paused and sniffed his hands. "I smell like pine. Give me a minute to wash up. I'm afraid, though, that you'll find the life and times of a geeky teen kinda boring."

Was he yanking her chain or was he oblivious to his own charm? She'd run the gamut with guys through her teens and endured all the fix-up attempts with sons, cousins, or whatever, of her parents' friends. For the most part they'd been toney, polished guys and often used the same clichéd come-on lines. It wasn't until she was in college that she made her own choices regarding male companionship.

From what she'd heard about Mike over the years during her visits to Watertown, he was considered shy, cute, and a catch, but very elusive. If he'd given her more than a passing glance back then, he would have caught *her* attention.

She flipped the page on Grandma's recipe folder and gathered ingredients for the next batch.

"Want some water?" Mike held up another bottle.

"Sure, let me get things ready for the next batch and I'll join you by the tree. Will you please hit play again? I intended to upgrade that CD player this year, but got busy and forgot."

"I like the songs."

Sam removed the wrapping from a stick of unsalted butter to let it soften. "Me too, the old ones say Christmas to me. Newer songs or redone versions of old ones, not so much."

Mike raised his water bottle in a toast. "Bing can be underrated."

The embers in the fireplace smoldered, and the tiny white lights on the tree filled the corner with a soft glow. Sam dropped into a chair and took a deep breath. "Thanks." She smiled at Mike when he handed her a bottle of water. "You did okay with the lights. Sorry if I hovered."

"I've been a victim of tree decorating hovering before. I'll live."

"Who? Who hovered in your past?"

"My sister, mostly. She's about as anal as you are about how things are done when decking the halls, the tree, etc. Janie could be a real pain about things." He repositioned a couple of the tiny lights, tucking them deeper in the fragrant branches.

Sam tipped her water bottle up and sipped, observing him as she screwed the top back on. His complaint about his sister held more nostalgia than annoyance. "I'm sorry, Mike."

Frowning, he shot her a puzzled look. "About what? And that's the second time you've apologized."

"The second?"

"Yeah, right after we'd patched up Al you said something about not meaning to insult me."

"Oh, that apology was for the remark about your smile. The second is for screwing up Christmas for you, for your family." She set the bottle aside and pushed out of her chair to seek the warmth of the fireplace. She lifted one of the fireside tools and poked the hot coals.

Mike followed and stood beside her, hands shoved into his pockets. "Neither apology is necessary. If you want to blame someone, blame the driver of the rig that dumped a moose onto the road. Shit happens, Samantha. I'm sure my sister won't be a bit upset if I'm not there pacing

76

with my buddy Al while she delivers my new niece or nephew. As for the smile remark, in case you haven't noticed I'm not a kid anymore. I've learned to take remarks about my less than perfect smile in stride."

The scent of lemon cookies mingled with holiday evergreen. As he stood beside her his warm, spicy scent mingled with the lemony scent coming from the baking cookies, tempting her to take a nice, healthy bite out of the man instead of a lemon Christmas cookie.

"A lot of teenage girls back then teased you because they *liked* your smile. I liked it, too. Still do. Your smile is endearing, memorable and as tempting as cookies."

He draped his arm over her shoulder and gave her a little squeeze. "Huh, really? I didn't think a guy with a crooked-toothed smile was tempting."

Sam relaxed against him. When he held her near things didn't seem so bad, but more than likely he was just being friendly. "You just didn't understand teenage girls back then."

"Back then? I don't understand girls, women, and at times old ladies, now. Why would I have been better at it as a hormonal teenager? I don't remember seeing you much after our initial meeting that time under the tree."

"Probably because I *wasn't* memorable, and I spent my visits at Christmas and during the summer hanging out with Grandpa at his office or at this cabin hiking the woods."

"Then how did you know about all these girls lusting after me?"

She chuckled and tapped the side of her head. "Ears to the ground, and my best source, Lil."

"Brown's Supply Lil?"

"Yep. From the time I met you under that tree, I was... interested, I guess you'd say. You had tears in your eyes, though you tried to hide them, but that told me a lot about you."

"Hmm, I did my best to hide those tears. I guess I really don't get how girls think." He took the poker from her hand and knelt to poke life into the coals before standing and setting the poker aside. "So, what did it tell you about me?"

"It told me you had a soft heart. Still do," she added. "Why didn't you use all that soft-hearted charm on girls?"

"I guess charming girls wasn't a skill I knew much about back then." He winked at her. "Maybe I've gotten better."

He grasped her hand and pulled her onto the sofa beside him. Startled, she stiffened. He draped his arm over her shoulder again. "Relax, I don't bite."

Feeling a bit foolish for acting so rigid, she leaned against him. He shifted, bringing her closer and smooth as silk, used his free hand to tip her chin up.

Their gazes caught and held.

Flickering firelight cast his face in shadow. Motionless under his quiet green-eyed gaze, her heart thumped in her chest.

He lowered his mouth to hers and Sam murmured, "I think you've aced the charm test."

The timer on the stove dinged.

Mere inches apart, Mike grinned, and his lips brushed hers when he spoke. "I think I hear bells."

Chapter Thirteen

"Done," Sam declared. Before Mike could react, she was up and gone, leaving him with empty arms. He pushed off the sofa, so much for his new-found charm.

Cheeks flushed, she shot a fast smile over her shoulder as she pulled the latest batch from the oven. "Why don't you finish decorating the tree? Then we can reward ourselves with fresh baked cookies."

Cookies weren't the reward he had in mind. Resigned, he reached for more decorations, and Sam continued her baking marathon.

Between batches she dashed back and forth helping, no *instructing*, him as he hung decorations. Her attempt to be... diplomatic, he guessed, didn't bother him. He found it rather amusing the way she'd maneuver him into decorating the tree *her* way.

And damn, these people had a lot of decorations. Handling the delicate glass ornaments made him sweat. Finally, he sank into a chair, resting his elbows on his knees. "I'm ready for a break."

"Come on, Mike. All we have left are these colored beads."

He wiped the back of his hand across his brow, frowning at the colorful strings of glass beads nestled in tissue. "I think you'd better handle this part. They look way too delicate for me."

"Can you get the last batch of chocolate chips when they're ready?"

"I can manage that." He rose and rolled up his sleeves. "Sturdy hot pan vs delicate glass beads. It's a no brainer."

While washing up for his kitchen duty, Mike glanced at the clock. "Hey, it's almost four o'clock. How about some more wine?"

Biting her lip, Sam wore a concentrated frown as she draped beads amongst the heavily laden branches. The tree glowed. Mike leaned back against the counter and took in the full effect.

She adjusted the drape of shiny blue beads and stepped back, surveying her work. "Sure," she said, with an absent glance toward him. She lifted the last strand from its bed of tissue. "Wine sounds good. White this time if that's okay. There's a back-up fridge with wine and beer in the pantry."

He checked the timer and followed her directions to the pantry down the hall. The tiny room was well stocked with supplies, everything from paper towels to well-marked jars of spices. Come to think of it, for a remote cabin in the woods this one had all the comforts of home.

Except for a TV. His hopes for catching up with the outside world had been dashed when Sam informed him there was no cable hook up for the twenty-six inch TV he'd discovered. The TV was an old CRT and, according to Sam, worked fine. Her eyes had glowed when she showed him a huge stack of old VCR tapes that he suspected included every Christmas movie ever produced.

He perused the white wine selection. "Hmmm, what goes with cookies and is appropriate for watching the black and white version of *Miracle on 34th Street*?"

Clutching two bottles, Mike strolled back into the main room just as the timer dinged. He set the wine on the counter and removed the cookies from the oven.

Sam joined him in the kitchen. "Pinot Grigio is one of my favorites." She picked up the second bottle and studied the label. "What's this one?"

"German Spatlese," said Mike. "I've had it before. It's crisp, and I think it will go well with chocolate chippers."

They settled on the sofa with a plate of warm cookies and a glass of chilled wine. The room smelled of pine, lemon, and chocolate. A hint of vanilla wafted from flickering thick white candles on the mantle, and the finished tree was magnificent.

Mike filled their glasses and then wedged the bottle of Spatlese into an ice bucket on the floor. He snagged a warm cookie. "We're eating cookies before dinner with wine. I feel like a kid."

Sam lifted her glass and touched it to his. "Reward for a job well done, and kids don't drink wine." She sunk back on the generous cushions and sipped, gazing at the tree. She'd turned off all but a small light in the kitchen. The tree lights created a soft glow as dusk darkened the white landscape outside the windows.

Mike relaxed and savored that first sip. They'd gotten through the day, and tomorrow was Christmas Eve. He turned to Sam. Faint frown lines creased her forehead.

She'd put on a good front all day, but at times he'd caught hints of moisture in her pretty blue eyes as she hung delicate glass balls on the tree. Each ornament must hold memories and remind her that the grandfather she loved could still be in danger.

When she'd informed him teenage girls had found him infatuating back in the day, he'd been surprised... and amused.

He reached over, trailed a finger down her arm. "Sam."

"Hmm?"

"Did you mean it when you said Cindy Devore really had the hots for me?"

"I did. I often overheard her," she added, grinning at him. "She complained she couldn't get your attention because you were always with Al Murray. For whatever reason, she hated your sidekick."

"Damn, and Cindy had a nice pair of... ah, eyes."

Chewing her first bite of cookie, Sam rolled her eyes. "Right, and at sixteen you had a thing for nice eyes."

He took a hefty bite of his cookie, gestured with his wine glass as he chewed and mumbled, "You have beautiful eyes."

*****

The CD clicked off. How should she respond? Was his compliment meant to be teasing and innocent? Sam focused on the glittering tree lights, lifted her glass and took a slow sip. The tang of Spatlese mingled with cookie sweetness.

Mike's voice cut through the lingering silence. "Sam, you've got chocolate, right here." He tapped the corner of his mouth.

She reached up, but Mike snatched her hand.

The contact sent a rush of warmth through her. He'd touched her before. They'd even shared a kiss without her system going into shock. Maybe it was the flickering firelight and the glittering Christmas tree that made this time different and... No, this was more.

She'd sensed it from the moment they'd reconnected and couldn't deny the heated tingle of attraction building between them.

He set his wine aside, curled his fingers around the nape of her neck, and then leaned forward and kissed her.

Sam's mind scrambled. He released his gentle hold on her and slid his hands down her arms, brushing the side of her breasts. This wasn't teasing *or* innocent, this was sweet and tart. Like Spatlese and chocolate, only better.

She shivered.

His arms slipped around her, pulling her closer. "Are you cold?"

Words lodged in her throat, and her pulse skipped like a stone over still water.

Cold?

How could she possibly be cold?

She fought to unjumble her chaotic thoughts. If she backed away, he'd release her without question. Yesterday *he'd* called a halt, claiming the time wasn't right. Now, with his breath warm on her skin there'd be no stopping unless *she* called a halt.

They'd reached an inevitable turning point. She drew in a deep, shuddering breath. "No, I'm anything but cold, and I have to admit you were right."

"I'm right about a lot of things. Could you be more specific?" His lips brushed her skin as he spoke.

Goosebumps spread over every inch of Sam's exposed skin, and she struggled to wrap her head around a response. "Specific, okay," she managed at last. "Wine and chocolate, they're perfect together. You were right."

"Hmmm, I agree. What else?"

"Timing."

81

"Timing? Like having wine and cookies *before* dinner?"

Her cheeks flushed and she choked out a weak laugh. "No, not having cookies before dinner. You turned me down yesterday and blamed your decision on timing."

"It was a tough decision."

She pulled back until their gazes locked and held. "Serious decisions are tough."

He raised his hand and cupped her cheek. "And this *is* serious, Sam, time for you to decide."

She covered his hand with hers, leaned forward and...

A deep, long low guttural cry stopped her cold. She dropped her hand, pulled away and shoved to her feet.

"Sam, wait! What the hell?" Mike caught up as she reached the door and slapped his hand against it, preventing her from opening it.

"Don't you hear him? Let me go!" she yelled and jammed her elbow into his side.

"Hold it, stop and think, damn it," he ground out and yanked her away from the door.

The harsh call, followed by several short, deep coughs came again.

"Mike, please." Sam's chest heaved with each breath. "Something's wrong. I have to get to him."

He dragged her several feet from the door. "Calm down," he ordered, giving her a shake. "We'll check it out together, but not before I get my gun."

She struggled, prying at his fingers. "You're hurting me."

His grip loosened. "Sorry. Can I trust you to wait? If he's hurt, another minute won't matter. If it's something else being armed could make one hell of a difference."

"Then hurry. That's a distress call. He's in trouble."

Mike turned her to face him. "Stay, and for God's sake, wait for me."

She gave a jerky nod. "Just hurry."

*****

Within seconds Mike returned. He'd shrugged into his coat and clipped a holster to his waist. He hurried toward Sam, his hand on the butt of the compact automatic in that holster. One hand on the latch, she waited.

He took her by the shoulders and positioned her behind him. "I go first, you get the lights." There was enough daylight that they could still move easily around the cabin's interior, but the windows in the barn were shuttered and it was bound to be as dark as a damn dungeon.

He pushed open the door. Hooves thudded on the hard packed floor and when Sam hit the overhead light, the agitated moose thrust his head over the top rail of the stall and let out another low, throaty call.

Arms thrust forward and locked, gun in hand, Mike swung left to right, ready to neutralize any threat within the shadowed stable. Nostrils flaring, audible pants came in quick succession from the distressed moose.

Mike lowered his weapon, but kept it front and center ready to engage if necessary. "Stay here," he ordered Sam. "I'm going to check the door first."

He stole a hasty look at Sam. Her face was chalk-white and her back was pressed against the wall beside the door. "Sam?"

"I'm all right. Go." Her eyes, open wide and unblinking, glittered ice blue under the harsh overhead light.

A thin line of powdery snow had sifted through the crack along the bottom of the outside door. "Damn loose latch," he muttered. Yet it appeared their makeshift latch was holding. There was no evidence that anything had entered the barn through that door.

He turned and started toward the stall, pointing a stiff finger at Sam when she stepped forward. "Hold it. Let me check inside the stall, and then you can check Al."

She frowned, but stopped and waited, arms crossed, shoulders hunched. The barn was freezing cold, and she wasn't wearing a coat.

He slid the stall door open and stepped inside.

Head raised, eyes flashing white, the moose backed away. He let out more rough coughs, but none of the louder distressed moans they'd heard moments before.

Still gripping the gun, Mike squatted low to check every dark corner of the stall. Satisfied, he straightened. He turned to leave the stall and smacked hard into Sam.

"Damn it."

"Sorry, sorry, I couldn't wait any longer." She peered around him. "Is he all right?"

"It appears so." He wrinkled his nose and lifted one arm, covering his nose. "God, it smells in here. If my room smelled this bad I'd be moaning, too."

She nudged him aside and entered the stall. Al moved deeper into the shadows. "Easy, fella. What spooked you?"

Mike backed up a couple steps. "How do you know he was spooked? Maybe he wants his stall cleaned the hell out."

Sam crouched down, kinda like he'd done moments before. "I don't see any fresh blood on his bandage. That's a good sign."

Mike gazed down at her. Her shoulders shook and she crossed her arms again, hugging herself tight. He stepped forward, reached down and hauled her to her feet. "Get inside and warm up. I'll stoke the wood burner and take a better look around. I think whatever upset him is long gone. Could be it was only his darned imagination. If a moose *has* an imagination," he muttered, and made Sam laugh.

"I am cold," she admitted. "I'll go and ... hey, are you all right?"

The room tilted and Mike grabbed the top of the stall. He slid his weapon into its holster and blew out a long, slow breath. "I think I moved too fast when I helped you up."

She stepped close and took his face between her hands. They were ice cold and he flinched.

"Hold still, let me look at you," she ordered.

Pain radiated from the injury on his forehead. He'd almost forgotten about it. In the past twenty-four hours his symptoms had all but disappeared.

Sam dropped her hands. "Let's get you back inside. Can you make it? Are you dizzy?"

He released his grip on the top rail and took a deep breath, relieved when the room didn't spin. "Yeah, I'm okay. Like I said, I think I moved too fast. You forget, all we had for supper was cookies and wine."

She closed the stall door and her arm came around him, guiding him toward the door to the cabin. "You could be right. I also know a concussion can appear to be healed and then symptoms reoccur. We're not taking any chances. You need to eat something and then rest."

"We do need food and rest," Mike agreed, and added, "Both of us. He draped his arm around her shoulder and together walked through the door into the cabin's warmth.

Chapter Fourteen

Feet tucked beneath her, Sam curled into a fireside chair. She gripped a mug of hot tea with both hands and studied Mike. He'd added several logs to the fire, stretched out on the sofa and fallen fast asleep. They'd both eaten and he'd downed a couple Advil, claiming the food and pills had taken care of his headache and any dizziness.

She'd checked his eyes. '*No*', he'd insisted, the light did *not* bother them. She got the same answer when she asked if sounds or noise irritated him. He'd given her that crooked grin and complained the only noise irritating him was *her*, asking so many questions. Though there hadn't been much heat behind his complaint.

Sam shifted her gaze back to the fire. Usually a crackling fireplace and full tummy was a recipe for sleep, as proven by the prone man on the sofa. Her body was tired, exhausted actually, but her mind would not shut down.

It was almost dark, and the upcoming night stretched long and endless before her. She finished the last of her tea and took her empty cup to the sink. There was nothing to do but rinse it out and set it aside. The dishes were washed, leftovers put away. She couldn't bake any more without disturbing Mike.

Heaving a deep sigh, she decided maybe a warm shower would relax her and was about to head to the bathroom when Mike's comment about the condition of Al's stall popped into her head.

Something physical might tip the scale and make her tired enough to fall asleep. Shoveling out a dirty stall fit that bill. One last check after slipping on her boots and a vest assured her Mike was down for the count. Pulling the door shut behind her, Sam entered the barn and flipped on the light.

First she checked on Al. He was tucked into the far corner and looked over with wary eyes when she slid the stall door open. "You can't sleep either, huh."

She wrinkled her nose. "Fresher air in here might help. Just stay put, Al. I'm going to get a shovel and make this stall more livable."

Her grandfather kept a sturdy wheelbarrow and tools in a separate room at the rear of the barn. She found them with no trouble, along with several bales of straw. "Leave it to you, Grandpa, to keep things stocked."

She hefted one bale into the wheelbarrow and returned to the stall. The heavy duty tire rolled soundlessly across the floor. She'd already worked up a sweat and paused to take off her thermal vest. Once inside, she removed a flat edged shovel balanced on the straw.

Al eyed her movements, his feet restless, but he remained in his corner. "Good boy," she crooned, and talked in a low voice as she shoveled and scraped. The job wasn't as thorough as she'd have liked, but most of the soiled straw was gone when she was done. She rolled the smelly load to the back door and returned to spread clean straw.

Nose to the ground, Al inspected her job. He emitted a couple soft grunts and took a drink of the fresh water she'd provided before easing down onto his clean bed. He was down, but he wasn't relaxed. His big ears twitched, swiveling each time the wind gusted and the barn walls creaked and shuddered.

Every muscle ached as Sam slid the stall door shut. The air was much fresher, but leaving the soiled bedding parked by the door wasn't a good idea. Tired to the bone she'd have no trouble falling asleep, and now she *really* needed that warm shower.

Feet dragging, she approached the outside door. From the rear of the barn a path led to a spot just inside the tree line where manure was dumped. A kind of compost area they'd developed. That path was no doubt clogged with snow and impassable. Her goal was to make it a few feet from the door and dump the load. Clean up would have to wait until the snow melted or the tractor in the garage equipped with a plow opened the path.

Grandpa used that plow every winter. Faced with the painful reality that this year was different gave her an empty, achy feeing deep inside. Overcome with an almost paralyzing sadness Sam paused.

"Think positive, darn it," she admonished and went to retrieve the vest she'd shed earlier. It would be smart to get her coat from inside the cabin, but she was so darned tired, now, and just didn't want to take the time. Besides, the chance of getting very far from the door was minimal. That wheelbarrow wasn't made for traveling in snow.

Plus, she hadn't forgotten about the wolf. She'd leave the door open and get out and in as fast as possible.

She zipped up the vest, pulled on gloves and grasped the door latch. Before lifting the latch she leaned in, her ear almost touching the rough wood, listening. Earlier Mike had checked the door, but he hadn't checked *outside* the door.

Since the wolf had disappeared into the woods they'd not heard his howl, which didn't mean a thing. Wolves were often quiet hunters. She glanced toward the stall and Al's head appeared over the top rail. He stared at her in silence.

She took a deep breath, undid the roping Mike had fashioned and lifted the latch. The door swung outward. A hard shove was needed to open it wide enough to get the wheelbarrow through the opening. Snow sifted down, coating the load she pushed. An overhang about eighteen inches wide protected her from the full force of the falling snow.

Almost through the door she stopped. "Damn," she muttered, and reached behind her, groping for the switch just inside the door. Her hand bumped the box and she flipped it on. Outside there were two small lights, one on each side of the door. Light from them created a pale orange glow in the darkness.

She pushed the heavy load out the door. The wheelbarrow plowed through the snow. It surprised her how far she went before a waist high drift brought her to a halt. A hearty shove drove the wheelbarrow's front end deep into the drift another two feet. Taking a deep breath, Sam lifted the handles and heaved the load into the snow. It tipped sideways but got the job done.

Ramming the loaded wheelbarrow into the snow was a piece of cake compared to hauling it back out. Snow that flew like powder when she'd hit the drift was packed like wet cement around the wheel. As she struggled to pull the empty cart out of the drift, behind her one light flickered and blinked out.

The remaining light was the farthest away, leaving her struggling in almost total darkness six to seven feet from the protective overhang, a lot further than she'd planned to venture. A sudden gust of wind rounded the corner and snow enveloped her. Blinded by the force of driven snow, Sam ducked her head.

Smacked by the wind she lost her grip and crashed into the snow, landing on her backside. Snow filled her boots, and as she floundered like a turtle on its back, snow managed to work its way under her vest and up her sleeves.

"Damn it"

Trying to do something useful had turned to crap. She was freezing, and as she rolled onto her hands and knees, the barn door banged shut.

No!

If the latch caught, she'd be stranded. The temperature was close to freezing, the wind chill was life threatening and her lifeline was sound asleep inside.

She sat back on her heels, brushing snow from her arms. The thermal shirt under her sweater was great when covered by something waterproof, but the vest left her arms exposed. Snow clung to her sweater, and bare skin exposed between it and her gloves burned like fire. Brushing the snow from her arms was futile. As fast as she removed it more fell, coating her head and shoulders. In front of her the barn loomed, a dark wall in a sea of white, and behind her the wheelbarrow lay on its side. The heavy odor of manure tainted the air.

She'd broken her own survival rules by not wearing proper gear and she hadn't propped the door open. Thank goodness, the other light stayed lit and the barn was still visible. She was almost afraid to blink or turn away, lest she lose sight of it and hoped the faint trail she'd left would lead her back to the door.

Rising to her knees, she was about to push to her feet when movement caught her eye. She turned her head and narrowed her eyes, searching the darkness. There, something was right there, and it was moving in her direction.

Icy fingers crawled up her spine.

Crouched next to the tipped cart, she tensed, ready to fight for her life as the unmistakable head and shoulders of the wolf emerged from the shadow of the barn.

The bottom dropped out of Sam's stomach in a sickening rush.

*****

Mike bolted upright. His heart rapped against his ribs and he gasped, struggling to breathe. The fire cracked like rifle fire and a log split, thudding onto the grate and sending a shower of sparks up the chimney.

Except for the glow from the fireplace the room was pitch black.

He kicked the throw aside and swung his feet to the floor. Other than the crackle and hiss of the dying fire, there was silence.

"Sam?" He pushed to his feet and paused, listening. "Where are you?" he called out a little louder.

Nothing.

The room lay deep in shadows, but he'd been there long enough to make his way across the room. He hit the switch and the overhead light came on. A swift look around revealed no smiling, freckle-faced woman, and every instinct Mike possessed went on alert.

Something wasn't right.

His gaze swept the undisturbed room, and flipping lights as he went, he made his way down the dark empty hallway. He checked every room and by the time he'd returned to the kitchen he was not only worried, he was steaming mad. If that stubborn woman had returned to the barn alone without bothering to tell him she was in for a big surprise.

He yanked his coat off the hook. It was chilly in the cabin and he knew damn well it would be freezing out there unless she'd kept the wood burner going. He wasn't taking any chances.

As he zipped his coat, angry as he was, he couldn't shake the feeling that he was missing something. Call it a sixth sense, or whatever, but it prompted him to retrieve his weapon before he entered the barn.

The air inside was cool and the light was on. Al paced inside his stall, pausing only once to stare at Mike before he resumed pacing, giving a low coughing grunt as he moved.

Sam was nowhere in sight. His gaze swept the area and when he saw snow spread across the floor just inside the rear door, adrenaline surged through his system. Wind shook the door, rattling the latch.

Had she lost her mind? What would possess her to go out by herself and not tell him? His mind raced as he crossed the room, gun in hand. He snagged an emergency flashlight, tucked it beneath his arm and grabbed the latch.

The fricken' handle came loose in his hand. "Son-of-a-bitch," he muttered, and his pulse kicked into high gear. He tossed the broken latch aside and used his shoulder to shove the door open. Wind and snow blasted through the opening knocking him back. He ducked his head, bracing his back against the door as he fumbled the flashlight into his hand and flipped it on. He extended both arms, flashlight in one hand, sidearm in the other, and swept the beam side to side.

The snow was blinding, and at first he saw nothing. His chest heaved and stomach-churning waves rolled in his gut. Gale force winds buffeted the door, slamming it against him like a battering ram.

"Sam!" he called out, "where are you?" The wind whisked his words away and he tried again. "Sam, answer me." There was no reply, and fear seeped in, spreading like the relentless cold.

The light picked up a faint depression in the snow. Head bent, he stumbled forward, then stopped and straightened at the sound of a low cry. He aimed the flashlight to his right.

The shaft of light pierced the swirling white wall and Mike's heart lodged in his throat when he saw Samantha lying on the ground. Only her legs were visible. Relieved, he slogged forward through the snow, but as he got closer the shaky relief nosedived. Something large and dark was draped across her body, and her legs weren't moving. Mike played the light over the gruesome tableau. His throat slammed shut and every breath he took was like sucking air through dense cotton.

Blood.

There was blood everywhere. Dark spots and wide, thick streaks glowed red in the flashlights beam. Like a gruesome path, the bloody trail led straight to the huge body of a wolf, and Sam was pinned beneath the motionless beast.

His grip on his handgun tightened and he dropped to a crouch. "Sam, can you hear me?"

Only the howling wind answered. Raw and primitive, the smell of blood choked him. Animal blood?

Or, *God forbid,* human?

Mike dropped to his knees. Was he too late? He tensed when wind ruffled the animal's bloody coat.

Had it moved? Was it only the wind?

Had steely jaws choked the life from Samantha?

His vision wavered. He could taste, *actually taste,* the gut-wrenching smell, and his breath came so fast and hard he almost didn't hear her faint call.

"Mike, help... can't move... freezing." Her voice was weak, her words slurred, but she was alive.

He dropped the flashlight and shoved the gun into his waistband. It was too dangerous to fire. He couldn't risk the round passing through the damn wolf and hitting Sam, which left him one choice.

He lunged forward and grasped the wolf's coarse scruff. With every ounce of strength he possessed, he yanked the body up and flung it aside. Off balance, he fell backwards into the snow. He fumbled for his weapon and took aim. Then it hit him. He rolled to his knees and slowly lowered the gun. Glazed over, the animal's eyes stared, open and fixed.

The damn wolf was already dead.

His gaze shot to Sam. He re-tucked his weapon into his waistband, and then crawled on hands and knees to her side.

He pulled off one glove and laid his hand against her pale cheek. Her lips were white, her eyes were closed and snow clung to her lashes. "Sam, can you hear me?"

She didn't respond. Her skin, so cold, it almost hurt to touch her. "Sam, honey, open your eyes. I've got to get you inside."

He ran his gaze over her. Her clothes were covered with blood, and it had already started to freeze. He skimmed his hand over her, looking for ... what? Bites, ripped flesh... *some* kind of wound. If he moved her and she was injured... he shook his head. Hypothermia was a killer, and her temperature had to be dangerously low. He slid his arms under her legs and shoulder. "Damn it, I have no choice."

He lifted her, gathered her close and started to move, his mind laser focused on reaching the barn. Its door banged in the wind and he kicked it aside, staggering into the barn.

His legs threatened to buckle as Sam hung limp in his arms. He cast a frantic look around, searching for someplace to lay her. The unlatched door banged closed, then open, and snow burst into the barn. He needed to get her into the cabin and get her warm, but he must secure the door.

He rushed to the door leading into the cabin, cradling Sam to his chest. He glanced down. Oh God, so much blood. He eased her onto the floor. He touched her neck, but his hand was shaking so bad he couldn't find a pulse. A quick hitch in his gut forced nausea up his throat.

Then her eyes fluttered open and his breath shuddered out. Her eyes closed again, but he'd seen life and detected the slight rise and fall of her chest. "Sam, wake up. Look at me."

She moaned and moved one arm. Her throat worked, as if trying to swallow. "Can't feel anything," she mumbled.

"Try and stay awake. I'll be right back, just wait."

She gave a barely discernable nod, and he leaped up and raced to secure the slamming door.

Chapter Fifteen

One minute movement jostled her. Then the next she seemed to float in a fog.

A cold fog.

Sam had never been this cold. She floated, as if drifting in an ice filled lake, fighting drowsiness that threatened to suck her under undulating frosty waves. She tried to focus on Mike's voice. His words faded in and out, broken sentences that made no sense in her muddled brain.

"Wait?"

He'd asked her to wait. She tried to smile and it hurt. She tried to nod and nothing happened. What else could she do but wait?

She inhaled, a shuddering breath, and the smell of straw and earth filled her head. *The barn.* She lay on the barn floor. Did Mike put her there? Why? Why would he do that?

Thoughts buzzed in her head.

Her breath caught. Mike was back, and his words as he lifted her made no sense. He pressed his cheek to hers, so warm, yet rough, not smooth. They were moving, every step a painful jolt.

She forced her eyes open, and then closed them against a blast of light. Caught up in a frigid, ghostly dream nothing seemed real. He lowered her onto something soft. Not the floor this time, but someplace warmer. Again, she forced her eyes open. Mike's back was to her. He knelt close by, and a red glow surrounded the outline of his body.

He glanced around, and then crawled to her on his hands and knees. His voice broke when he cupped her face and rested his forehead on her. "Thank God, you're awake."

She cried out when he removed his hands, taking the warmth away.

"Shhh, it's okay. You'll be okay, but Sam, I've got to get these wet things off of you."

He touched her, murmuring softly as he tugged wet clothes from her frigid skin. He eased the sodden thermal over her head, tugged clinging jeans down unfeeling legs.

Gathering her trembling body into his arms, he pulled her onto his lap and covered her with something soft and dry. Heat from his body drew her like a magnet, and she pressed against him.

She began to shiver, teeth rattling spasms that shook her head to toe, and between bouts of her body shaking uncontrollably, awareness to her surroundings began to come into focus.

Deep lines creased Mike's forehead as he scowled down at her. She

91

moved her toes, cringing when pain shot through her feet. At some point he must have removed her boots and socks along with her wet clothes. She didn't care. All she wanted was to burrow against his warm body and sleep.

"Sam, try to stay awake." Her head rested on his chest and his voice rumbled in her ear.

"I'm so cold. I want to sleep and I keep shivering."

"Shivering is good, Sam, but you've got to try and stay awake. You're borderline hypothermia."

She gazed up at him through lowered lashes, and he tucked the warm throw tighter around her, pulled her tighter against him. Welcome warmth seeped into her. More alert now, she took inventory. With great effort she moved her arms and legs. She sucked in deep breaths and then forced her eyes open.

Mike's face came into sharper focus, and she realized they were on the couch in front of a roaring fire. He bent forward and straightened with a bottle of water in his hand. He held it to her lips. "Drink. You need fluids."

Tepid water filled her mouth. Deprived tissues in her throat sucked it up like a sponge.

"Not too much," he said. "Small sips to start."

Sam rubbed her lips together after a second drink. Her breathing evened to a more normal pace and her skin warmed. Her *naked* skin.

Her eyes snapped wide open. "My clothes are gone."

He brushed wet strands of her hair from her cheek, frowning. "They were wet, soaked with... snow."

She tried to move her arms but found them trapped in the heavy throw covering them both. "Am I... do I have..."

"No, you're not naked. You still have on panties and a... ah bra." A grin replaced the frown. "Despite the need to hurry, I couldn't help but notice that it's a very pretty, lacy bra, too."

She blinked, twice, but had no appropriate words to respond.

He chuckled. "Think of it as... medicinal, kind of an emergency measure." He tucked the throw tighter beneath her chin. "How are you feeling?"

Welcoming the change of topic, she averted her eyes and took a quick inventory. She could now move her fingers and toes without too much discomfort, but lifting her arms or moving her legs sapped her energy. "I'm tired and the thought of moving... I don't know if I could even stand right now." She shivered. "I'm starting to warm, but deep down in my bones, I'm still ice cold."

"Believe it or not, that's encouraging. I'd feared hypothermia, maybe even frostbite, but apparently you weren't out there long enough for either to get a grip. You're suffering from exposure, though. That's bad enough. You're going to be weak, no strength, and tired, but with some liquids and rest you'll be fine."

Her eyes drooped. "Okay. You're right. I can't keep my eyes open."

"Here, drink some more water and then you can take a short nap. Not too long." He brushed the back of his hand over her cheek. "After you rest we'll get some warm liquids into you. Then we'll talk about what happened out there."

A tiny frown creased her brow, but she nestled closer, wiggling a bit and settled against him. "Right now everything is fuzzy. Give me a couple minutes, okay, *Doctor Donovan*." Her eyes closed and she drifted asleep, warm and comfortable in Mike's arms.

*****

Mike stared at the ceiling. He took slow even breaths, trying to take his mind off the near naked woman all but wrapped around him. "Think medicinal," he muttered to himself, but unless she quit pressing into his lap with nothing between them but flimsy silk and denim, medicinal wasn't going to cut it.

Right now he was thankful the denim was containing a reaction she couldn't help but notice if she'd been running at full capacity.

He touched her cheek. Thank God her color was coming back. When he'd found her she'd been sheet white, her lips almost blue. It had been less than a half hour, more or less, and the reappearance of color meant there'd be no permanent skin damage. It takes about two hours to recover from exposure. He'd let her rest a bit, then he wanted answers.

He shifted, repositioning her in his lap.

Doctor Donovan. Her smart ass remark assured him she was recovering. He lifted his arm, checked the time. Was it only an hour ago he'd awakened to find her gone?

He slouched lower, resting his head on the puffy cushion behind his back. In a couple of hours it would be Christmas Eve, and bar none, this would be the screwiest holiday he'd ever experienced.

He wasn't with his family and the worst snow storm in his lifetime raged on outside. To top things off, curled up sleeping in his lap was a woman he'd not seen much of since childhood. Today he'd seen *too* much because not a lot covered the curvy body he'd glimpsed briefly while racing to save her life.

Okay, maybe it *was* more than a glimpse. He's only human, damn it.

Before the mad dash through a blizzard to save that fine body, there'd been a shift. A definite change in the... interaction, he guessed for lack of a better word, between them.

She had some explaining to do, though. Just when he'd changed his mind about her being a scatter head, she'd smashed his new found respect to smithereens. He wanted an explanation. The hell of it was how he'd get one without tramping all over her shaky self-esteem.

And once he got that explanation, how would it affect feelings between them that he knew damn well had intensified after the *shift*.

The fire dwindled and Mike dozed. Night was closing in, and soon he'd have to wake Samantha and check her out.

She stirred and breathed a long, low sigh. Her eyes fluttered open and she gazed up at him. A drowsy smile curved her lips. "Hi."

"Hi, sleepyhead, I was about to wake you. How do you feel?"

"I'm still not quite warm, especially my hands, my feet." She scrunched up her face. "How long did I sleep?"

"Overall, about two hours, give me your hands," he said, and slid his beneath the throw, surprised to find hers still icy cold. He wrapped his around them, and when she intertwined her fingers with his he sucked in a quick breath. The move had trapped his hands, pressing them to her warm, smooth, belly.

She went very still. Her eyes were wide open now and very aware as her gaze locked with his.

*****

Everything fell into place, much like an old movie playing through her mind in jerky scenes. He'd come for her and in a quick flash she remembered his face, rigid and strained, as he'd lifted the wolf and tossed it aside. The rest filtered through, bits and pieces.

She'd rested, and though still shaky, was more alert than she'd been two hours ago. Only his words came back to haunt her now. He'd laid it all out and left no doubt that after rest and hot liquids he wanted an explanation of what had happened out there.

She closed her eyes. The warmth of his hands seeped into her like warm syrup. Mike had risked his life to save her -- again -- and it was up to her to make him understand why and how she'd put them both in danger.

"I'd like to take a shower and get dressed." She opened her eyes to find him staring down at her, his expression unreadable. Several beats passed, then he nodded slowly and released her hands. He tucked the throw around her, scooped her up and set her aside.

The gesture was abrupt, and the sudden loss of his warmth hit hard.

She shivered. Her arms weighed like anvils, her moves clumsy as she gathered the throw around her.

Mike got to his feet. He helped her stand, gripping her shoulders when she swayed. "Are you okay?"

The room tilted, and her knees almost buckled. She took a deep breath, curling her toes on the cool floor. At least now she could feel them. "I will be. Just give me a minute."

"I'll get you some clean clothes and put them outside the bathroom for you. It will be warmer there, and you can shower and dress without moving around much."

"Thanks." She slipped one arm out of the tangled folds and gripped his forearm. "I owe you so much and--"

He shook his head. "All I want is an explanation. That's all. This isn't about owing."

Her fingers tightened on his arm. "No, it isn't. It's more. Something's happening between us, Mike. Let's see if that something is worth pursuing, or best left alone."

Unflinching, she met his gaze. After a long moment, he repositioned her hand. "All right, I'll help you to the shower and get your clothes."

"I'll need something comfortable, sweats will do."

He walked beside her, and she clung to his arm for support. When they reached the bathroom she stepped inside. As he continued down the hallway, she called to him, "Mike."

He swung around and started back to her.

She raised one hand, palm out. "No, I'm fine. I wanted to make sure you get everything I need."

He paused, one brow lifted. Her heart twisted a little at the deep lines framing his tired green eyes. How did she not see the toll this day had taken on him?

She took a deep breath, and then mirroring his arched brow, smiled. "I'll need something for under the sweats," she reminded him and closed the door.

Chapter Sixteen

Mike stared at the closed door. Mysterious, puzzling, perplexing, all of the above didn't quite describe the effect of her parting smile.

A punch to the solar plexus nailed it, though.

He listened until the sound of running water assured him she'd made it into the shower. His feet dragged as he walked away, yet, a part of him pondered what she'd do if he yanked open the door, stripped, and joined her.

The woman baffled him. He wasn't about to get his heart stomped into a pulp. He wanted more, but damned if he knew what the hell *more* meant.

He tossed her duffle onto the bed and rooted around for sweats, amazed at how much she'd managed to stuff -- neatly, too -- into the LL Bean tote. He located a pair of dark blue sweats and matching pullover. "Nice blue. Blue is great with her eyes and... crap," he muttered, and tossed them onto the bed. "How can I be objective when every time I look into those eyes I feel like I'm drowning?"

And damn, her undergarments were blue too. Darker than her eyes, but he imagined the color would give them a hell of a boost. The silken fabric was trimmed in cream-colored lace, and his fingers turned all thumbs as he held up the delicate pieces. "I'm only doing what she asked me to do. I shouldn't feel like a damned pervert."

He stacked the sweats, plus a pair of heavy socks on the floor outside the bathroom door. With a smug nod, he put the undergarments right on top, and as the whirring hair dryer cut off, he tapped on the door. "Here's your stuff."

After a moment of silence came a soft, "Thank you."

"I'd like to take a shower, too. Will you be all right?"

"Yes, I'm fine. A hot shower really helped. I'll get dressed, get out of your way and go make some tea."

Once Sam was clear, clutching an oversized towel Mike entered the bathroom. A long, hot shower sounded like heaven. He glanced into the mirror and shot himself a wry grin. Maybe a cold shower would be wiser. He opted for hot, though, and the hot water eased stiff muscles but did little for the fatigue that had his tired butt dragging.

He poked into a closet and pilfered a clean pair of sweats that no doubt belonged to Doc Gates. Doc was trim, too, and they weren't a bad fit. Beneath the black pants and gray hoodie Mike wore his own tee shirt and skivvies. As he ran a brush through his damp hair, he hoped that Sam's grandpa wouldn't mind sharing his clothes.

The teapot whistled as he entered the kitchen and he hurried forward. He poured the boiling water into the waiting cup and glanced around when Sam hurried into the room.

"Oh, thanks. I was... ah, putting some clothes to soak in the back room. There's a washer and dryer there," she explained. "If you'd like to bring me your things I'll take care of them, too."

Mike glanced around the room. Missing were the wet, bloody items he'd stripped from her hours before. His coat was missing, too, and the boots sitting by the door, both hers and his, looked clean.

"You've been busy," he said, and reached for another cup. Might as well join her and have tea, too. It would give him something to do with his hands while she talked.

And he had no doubt she was going to talk. He just didn't know if he wanted to hear what she had to say.

She appeared well recovered and breezed past him to add milk and sweetener to her tea. "I added more logs to the fire after I checked on Al. Let's sit there." She grimaced. "I'm still a bit chilled."

"How is Al?" he asked. A close call with exposure hadn't knocked her down as much as he'd feared. He tossed the spent tea bag, and eyed her as he doctored his own tea. There were dark smudges under her eyes, and her hand shook as she took that first sip of tea. No, she still suffered. Fatigue dogged her every move.

Pure adrenaline, he figured. Sooner or later she'd crash, but it had pushed her to keep moving, to get things done. Things like making tea, checking on Al and taking care of blood soaked clothes. As she settled on the couch and stretched out long legs, her sigh was silent, but slumped shoulders and half closed eyes spoke volumes.

Mike was tempted to settle beside her, put his arm around her and let her talk. After a brief mental battle, he opted to keep his distance and dropped into the far corner of the couch.

With a puzzled frown she turned her head, facing him. The frown slid into a tired, resigned smile and she lifted her teacup in a mock toast. "I guess you're ready to hear my version of what went on out there."

Slouched in the corner he took a long, deliberate sip of hot tea. Then he lowered his cup and replied, "Whenever you're ready."

*****

Mike's low quiet voice unsettled her, and she almost wished he'd yell at her. She sipped her tea, and the hot liquid burned a path all the way to her belly. There was less than three feet between them, but it might as well have been three miles if the cool demeanor radiating from Mike was any measure.

Once again she'd given him reason to paint her with the brush of brainless. She smiled at her analogy. Not bad for an empty-headed woman. Changing that impression was up to her now. The hot shower had washed away rusty bloodstains on the surface. Inside, new self-awareness took hold.

She'd run each step she'd taken through her mind over and over. Should she have done things differently, maybe, but would it have changed anything? The truth was it made no difference now. She'd made a decision and acted, and darn it, she was ready to defend those actions.

If Mike's opinion of her suffered because of her choice, she'd deal with it. The bottom line was *she'd* made the choice. She hadn't hesitated or worried about 'what if', an attitude that had plagued her all her life. If nothing else, the past couple of days strengthened her self-confidence.

She no longer feared pursuing goals and, after considering risk, she'd make decisions and act. No more struggling to please like a guilt-ridden daughter. She'd move forward as a confident adult.

And when the timing was right, she'd move as a woman.

Clutching her cup with both hands, she angled her body to face Mike. "Why don't I start by explaining... No." She stiffened her spine, lifted her chin. "I don't have to explain my actions, but I will express how and why I made decisions based on what I had to deal with at the time."

Mike's eyes widened. She'd surprised him. Good, anything was better than the silent, cold distance between them.

She took a calming breath and cleared her throat. "I was exhausted. I could barely put one foot in front of the other, yet my mind wouldn't shut down. You'd fallen dead asleep. I envied you, knowing I'd just lay there wide-awake if I lay down.

"It had been a while since I'd checked on Al, so I decided to do that and load up the wood burner, too. I'd accomplish something and maybe wear myself down enough to sleep."

"So far, I'd agree with you," Mike stated. "It's what you decided later that I question."

"Before you jump in with opinions, consider this. Before you fell asleep you'd been fighting a headache. I asked a few medical questions, concerned about that blow you took to your thick skull."

"*My* thick skull?"

She ignored his affronted tone. "You said I was bothering you."

Mike's brows slammed together. "I was kidding. You were as tired as I was and--"

"You needed to rest. *I'm* not recovering from a concussion."

He clamped his mouth shut.

"You dropped off like a rock the minute your head hit the pillow and, not wanting to '*bother*' you, I went to check on my moose alone."

"Okay, I guess I wasn't very helpful."

Sam aimed a pointed look at him. "You guess?"

He opened his mouth, then closed it and shrugged.

Sam nodded and resumed talking. "I sensed Al was nervous as soon as I entered the barn. He was pacing, and every few minutes he'd stop and look at the back door. Every time wind rattled that door it sounded like it was going to burst open. The darn thing made me nervous."

Mike's fingers drummed on his thigh. "I meant to replace that latch."

"It wouldn't have changed anything. I'd already made up my mind. I was going to clean that stall."

"Okay, so far I can't argue with your decision."

"I'm glad you agree," she remarked, and in clipped tones relayed what she did up until she was ready to go dump the wheelbarrow.

Mike listened in silence until she reached that point. "Damn it, Sam. Did you think to look before you went outside?"

Her tea had grown cold, as cold as the chill spreading through her as she gathered her thoughts and braced to relive what had happened next. She set the cup aside. "Yes, of course I looked outside. I stopped and listened, too. All I heard was the wind. I could make out the path to the manure dump, even though it was covered with drifts. It started a couple feet from the door so I pushed the load forward as far as I could and unloaded. I was surprised when I turned around and saw how far I'd gone, but I didn't panic."

She shot Mike a challenging look and repeated, "I didn't panic, Mike. I was cold, but I was all right. I just wanted to get back inside."

A sudden chill made her turn to the crackling fire. Her insides tightened. Now came the hard part. The part where she'd faced driven snow and unbelievable cold alone.

Only she hadn't been alone.

"Then things went bad," she whispered.

Mike shifted, as if to move closer. She held up one hand and shook her head. "I'm all right," she assured and continued, her voice was still shaky but stronger. "The wolf... he'd been in the shadow of the barn and I didn't see him until he moved and came at me. As soon as he stepped into the light I saw the blood. His side, his back... he was covered with blood. I tried to get away but the snow was too deep. I fell."

Reliving the nightmare hit harder than she'd imagined. She hunched over and drew in a shuddering breath, staring at the dancing flames. Though the acrid scent of burning logs clogged her throat, she gathered her thoughts and continued

"The wolf kept coming, and I tried to get up. I couldn't. He kept getting closer and closer." Her eyes closed, reliving that horrible moment. She crossed her arms, hugging her body, shivering violently. "There was so damn much blood."

"Sam." Mike's voice shattered the image.

She blinked, turned and reached for him. His warm hands closed over her frigid fingers. "That's enough, Sam. Let it go."

"I have to finish this, Mike. I have to finish it once and for all."

His grip tightened. "I'm here, and I'm listening."

"He was staggering now," she continued, "and I saw how bad he was injured. I wasn't afraid any more. I was sad. It was almost worse than the fear because I knew that beautiful wolf was dying."

Tears blurred her eyes. "I tried to get up and the wind knocked me back. I must have fallen and hit my head against the wheelbarrow because everything went black. I don't know how long I was out, but when I woke I panicked because the wolf was on top of me and I couldn't move. I smelled his fur, and I smelled his blood. At first I didn't know he was dead. I was freezing, colder than I've ever been in my life. Then I realized he'd died, and I thought I was going to die too."

She started to shake and Mike pulled her into his arms. She burrowed against him. "I heard you calling me. I tried to answer but I couldn't get my breath. I was so scared."

"Shhh, enough, I heard you. I found you."

He held her, running his hand up and down her back as she clung to him. "I wanted to help him, Mike, but it was too late. He was torn to pieces and bleeding so badly and... "

He touched his lips to her brow. "It was too late long before you found him, Samantha. The first time we saw him we knew that something was wrong with him. A lone wolf, a sick wolf, doesn't stand a chance under good conditions. You couldn't have saved him, Sam. I'm sorry you had to see him die."

*****

He held her until she relaxed against him, breathing deep and even. She'd been through hell. Her decision to leave the safety of the barn was a bad one, yet given the same circumstances he may have done the same. Their career choices were alike in some ways.

As a federal wildlife officer he took risks and often bowed to the natural order of things.

As a vet she'd fight unwinnable battles because sometimes fate just took a turn and you lost.

Tonight she'd made a choice, a solid choice, not an impulse. She'd shed tears for a dying wolf, even reliving the horrible experience had drained her. Her heart would suffer.

Yet the experience didn't break her. He knew without a doubt she'd be stronger, she'd move on, and her heart would heal.

He dozed, and tried to keep his mind off what the woman in his arms wore beneath her soft blue sweats.

Much later he jolted awake. His left arm was asleep. After a fast assessment, he blinked away grogginess and shifted Sam's weight, setting off sharp tingles as blood flowed down his arms to his numb fingertips.

The room was cold and very quiet. Only embers glowed in the fireplace, so he understood the cold. The silence was kind of creepy until it hit him.

No wind pounded the cabin. Darkness pressed against the windows, but the sizzle of snow driven by gale force wind against the glass was gone.

Sam stirred in his arms. "This is becoming a habit," she murmured. Her face was hidden, burrowed into his chest, her words muffled.

"I've no complaints. Some habits bear keeping."

She lifted her hand, smoothing tangled hair from her face she peered up at him. She smiled and his breath caught. It was the same smile she'd sent him earlier just before she'd closed the bathroom door in his face. He had no clue what it meant.

Though a cat eyeing a bowl of cream came to mind.

So... he grinned and placed a chaste kiss on her forehead. "Do you hear it?" he asked.

Her brow creased and she went silent, listening he presumed. Then her smile spread. "Nothing. I hear nothing. Maybe the storm is over." She swung her feet to the floor and sat up. "Darn, it's cold in here."

Mike nudged her aside, reluctantly. "I'll get the fire going again."

Hunkered down, he added logs and poked the hot coals. Sam stood, stretched and then disappeared down the hallway. Bathroom, he figured, and added dry kindling. The tiny twigs caught and blessed heat bathed his face. He rubbed his eyes against a smoky backdraft, but then the wood caught and the flames carried the smoke up the chimney.

He stood and faced the hallway. Sam's soft humming made him smile, until she strolled back into the room wearing a coat. His response must have showed on his face because the humming cut off and she stopped. He recognized the stubborn jut of her chin as she pulled on her gloves. "I'm going to check on Al one more time tonight."

Mike bit his tongue and rubbed the back of his neck as he walked toward her. For one long moment, they stood facing one another.

He took a deep breath.

She arched her left eyebrow.

Lifting his hand, he traced her jawline with one finger. "Relax, Sam. Checking on Al's a good idea. I'll fix that broken latch while you check."

Her rigid stance softened. "Good idea." She headed for the door, then paused and glanced back at him. "I'll find the new latch. You know where Grandpa's tools are, and I'm there to help if you need me."

The door closed with a snap behind her and he rubbed his neck again. There was still tension between them. He'd just have to deal with it until they found a way to take the edge off.

Since his coat was in the wash, he once again 'borrowed' from her grandfather. He slipped on a well-worn jacket, humming as he imagined several scenarios guaranteed to take the edge off.

*****

"Almost done over there?" Sam slid the stall door closed.

"Almost," Mike replied. "The new latch is much better." He pushed against the door to test the chain and hook.

Sam strolled closer. "It looks good. I'll be inside. The wood stove is stoked and Al's set for the night."

Mike glanced at the moose, whose head rested on the stall's top rail. Water dripped from the dark, ungainly nose. "He looks pretty relaxed."

"A clean stall, water, and food equal all the comforts of home," she said, slanting a pointed look at Mike.

Their looks locked and held. He grinned. "No argument," he said, and began to put away tools. Sam left and returned to the cabin.

Christmas Carols played softly as she turned on the tree lights. She'd let a single light burning in the hallway and lit the fat white candles on the mantle. The fireplace blazed, warming the room. She touched the bump on her head where the wheelbarrow had caught her. The spot was tender, but a couple Advil had taken care of any discomfort.

She rehung a red ball that was about to slide off one of the tree's feathery branches. Her heart gave a little hitch when Mike had come into the barn wearing Grandpa's coat. The coat wasn't the only reason for the hitch. All Mike Donovan had to do was grin at her and her heart not only hitched, it hammered. She was well aware of Mike's effect on her, but did he feel the same in return? And that was a very interesting question.

She stepped back, running a critical eye over the tree. The door to the barn opened behind her. "All fixed, for now." The door closed and she waited while Mike hung up his jacket -- correction, Grandpa's jacket.

The back of her neck tingled as he approached behind her.

"I checked outside," he said, settling his hands on her shoulders. "The wind has stopped, and snow is falling straight down coating everything. Mother Nature's all set for the holiday. It's kinda pretty."

She eased back enough so the tip of his chin rested against her hair. Deliberate, yes, but a sure way to answer that very interesting question.

His hands slid down her arms and around her body, bringing her closer. Then he crossed his arms. The move anchored her against him.

She relaxed, letting the flow of music and the extra vanilla scented lotion she'd slathered on after her shower work its magic.

Candles flickered on the mantle and outside the window steady snow continued to fall. Big flakes now, drifting down, layering like soft cotton on the window's ledge.

After a long moment, he kissed her neck. "Are you warm enough?"

She angled her head, giving him better access. "Hmm, and getting warmer by the minute."

"Glad to be of service." He trailed his lips along the curve of her neck. "Are you well rested and relaxed?"

"Any more relaxed and I'll melt like candle wax." She turned, facing him, and wrapped her arms around his waist.

He linked his hands behind her, resting them on the curve of her hip. He kissed her forehead, each cheek and the tip of her nose before slanting his head and claiming her lips.

When the long, deep kiss ended, she rested her head on his chest. His heart thudded beneath her ear as his hands roamed up and down her back. Earlier the gesture had soothed and comforted, now it aroused.

Arms wrapped around one another they swayed, their feet barely moving, to the smooth, familiar tempo of White Christmas.

They moved in small circles, pausing to kiss, continuing when the CD selection changed. "Mike," she murmured.

He nuzzled against her neck. "Hmm?"

"I think it's time." She drew back and looked up. His eyes were half closed and a sleepy smile curved his lips.

"Time for what?"

She arched her brow, waiting.

His eyes flicked open, a flash of green. The music ended and only the simmering coals in the fireplace broke the silence.

She touched her lips to his. Then lay her hand on his cheek, gave it a gentle pat and slid from his embrace. She circled the room blowing out candles and turned at the entrance to the hallway. "Can you get the tree lights?"

Mike glanced at the tree, then back to Sam. "I can do that."

She nodded, turned and walked away. Her heart hammered in her chest and her knees trembled. What if he didn't follow her? Other than the flash of heat in his eyes, he'd appeared stunned. She stepped into the darkened bedroom and flipped on a nightlight.

Either the timing was right, or it never would be.

Chapter Seventeen

A fast detour netted protection. Necessary if the night was heading where Mike thought it was, and wise.

The bedroom was cool. He appreciated the coolness, because the fire raging inside him threatened to melt the skin off his bones.

He'd been working his way toward the same end result until she'd taken the lead. He had moves, a guy developed a rhythm. She'd trumped his moves, and the gentle seduction he'd pondered was left in the dust.

A nightlight burned low. His eyes adjusted and he scanned the room. He'd feel like an idiot if she wasn't... but ah, there she was, tucked under the covers. She lay on her side, hands folded beneath her cheek. Her eyes were open, her gaze fixed on him.

"You surprised me, Sam," he murmured as he crossed to the bed.

"I hope you like surprises." She smiled up at him.

Her decision came through loud and clear, but it was up to him to erase the nerves and uncertainty he sensed, despite her inviting smile.

Moving slowly, eyes locked with hers, Mike unzipped the hoody and shrugged out of it. When he turned to toss it onto a chair he saw the dark blue sweats she'd been wearing were already there. They were neatly folded and stacked just the way he'd done when he'd placed them in the hallway for her. The delicate, lacy undergarments were missing.

His gaze shot to Sam's.

Her come hither smile shot right back at him.

He peeled off his tee shirt. The sweatpants followed and when he straightened Sam had lifted the corner of heavy spread. "The room's cool," she murmured. "Join me?"

Without hesitation, he slid in beside her. Her warmth drew him like a magnet. He pulled her against him, skin to skin, and kissed her. Every curve, every angle was a perfect fit. Her scent, sweet vanilla like the candles, filled his head and she melted against him like hot candle wax.

His fingers skimmed over her shoulders, glided down the long, lean flow of her back. It was like touching warm silk, yet toned muscles rippled beneath his hands.

He broke the kiss. "Sam," he murmured.

"Hmmm?"

"Just, Sam," he said, and his gaze lowered to dark blue lace. His breath caught and he struggled, fighting a wild impulse to rip away that last barrier.

He skimmed a finger over the curve spilling from the lace, then lifted his gaze and cupped her face between his hands. "I need to catch my breath. I don't want to rush."

Her lips curved, and her hands slid up his chest. Mirroring him, she cupped his face. "Um, slow is good. It's been a while... and, I'm not very... experienced."

He rubbed his thumb against her cheek. Her eyes gleamed, blue crystal in the dim light. "Let me look at you, Sam."

He craved this woman like no other.

Why?

What made Samantha Gates different?

He'd been with women, and surely she'd been with other men. Yet he couldn't bear to think of anyone else holding Sam, *touching* her.

She took his hands. "The snap is in back," she whispered.

His mind raced and his blood headed south. At first he fumbled the clasp, but when he succeeded, she gave a soft hum and shrugged out of the lacy garment. His gaze lowered. "You're beautiful, despite what your mom thought," he blurted, then thought, *shit!*

Her soft laugh assured him she understood the reference and didn't hold it against him. But when his hands covered her, the laugh turned to a gasp, followed by a deep, shuddering sigh that nearly shattered his restraint.

She lowered her gaze, and his hands molded her curves. From across the room the nightlight's glow highlighted the curve of her shoulder, the outline of well-rounded breasts.

He skimmed his fingers over rigid peaks and she arched into his embrace. "I want to touch you, Mike."

He kissed the full swell of her breast. "Not yet. Just give me a little more time to know you."

Her hesitant admission -- 'it's been a while' and 'not very experienced' -- demanded he go slow. He'd been so intent, so stimulated he'd nearly jumped in and selfishly satisfied his own fierce need. He wasn't a hormonal teenager, damn it.

And this wasn't a conquest he'd walk away from unscathed.

"You already know me." Sam's gentle assurance soothed him, wrapped around him in the intimate darkness.

"Ah, there are many ways to know a woman."

He touched her, learning the curve of her hip, hoping to dispel nerves almost tangible as his hands skimmed over her. Her deep sigh turned to a long, low moan as he stroked down her body.

The decision to be with him had been hers. Yet her heart pounded beneath his intimate caresses. He hesitated. "Sam, are you sure? I don't want to rush--"

"I'm sure. I wouldn't be here with you if I wasn't." She took his hand, pressed it to her breast. "You relax me just because you're you."

"I want you aroused, Sam, not relaxed." He replaced the hand on her breast with his lips.

She sucked in a quick breath. "That works."

Her arms wound around his neck, pressing her naked body closer, trashing Mike's resolve to go slow. Breathless gasps became throaty moans as his mouth and hands grew bolder.

He brushed his palm over her belly and lower over the remaining triangle of blue lace. She lifted her hips, and he slid the last barrier away. The scent of their passion mixed with the sweet scent rising from her bare skin. Sweet vanilla he could almost taste laced with raw need filled his head, blurred his mind.

Her hands explored him, bolder now, more urgent as they tugged at *his* last barrier. He helped, shoving his skivvies down and tossing them aside. He stopped and cursed, almost forgetting one important step.

She reached for him when he lifted away. "Mike, where... oh."

Seconds later he pulled her beneath him. She arched, opened and sighed as they came together. Her fingers threaded through his hair, slid down his back, then pressed him to her so their hearts beat in unison.

Her body moved beneath him, gentle rolling waves taking him to the edge. Soft skin, soft curves surged against him and when his long, low, moan triggered her urgent cry of release, Mike let go and shattered.

*****

Sam lifted her hand, faltered, and let it fall. Every cell, every bone, every muscle in her body was limp. "Umm, don't move," she pleaded when Mike stirred and began to roll away.

"I'm afraid I'll crush you." Braced on his elbows he touched his lips to her forehead. "Relaxed, are you?"

She gazed up at him. Her eyes had adjusted to the darkness, and aided by the soft glow of the nightlight, his crooked grin twisted her heart. "I am. I like your method."

He slid to her side and tucked her back against him, wrapping his arm around her and covering one bare breast. She settled in, drifting, his body warm against her back.

"Are you going to conk out on me?" His voice rumbled in her ear.

"Maybe. You were shooting for relaxed, weren't you?"

He chuckled, his breath warm against her neck. "What did you mean when you said I relaxed you just being me? I'm flattered, I guess, but hoped I'd honed a few relaxing uh... techniques."

"I have no complaints about your technique. As for my comment, I guess I meant you appear to have an effect on me no other man does."

"Have there been many other men?" He gave a rough cough. "Sorry, scratch that. It was rude."

"No, it wasn't. I told you I wasn't experienced. Now I know it isn't experience, it's..."

"Technique?"

She chuckled. "My *first* experience was in college. The guy was a friend. I liked him. I felt safe with him. I didn't love him, nor did I fall in love with him during our brief encounter."

"How was his technique?"

"At that point in my life I guess I'd say pleasant."

"Pleasant? A back rub is pleasant."

His humor made her smile. His honest warmth melted her heart. Sam twisted onto her back, covering the hand he kept on her breast with hers. She looked into his eyes, glowing soft green in the shadowed room. "What just happened between us wasn't pleasant. When I said I was relaxed just because it was you I was prepared for pleasant. Now I know there's so much more."

She lifted her hand, rubbed her knuckles against his cheek. Bristles rasped against her fingers and muscles low in her belly clenched. "I like you, Mike. From the very first time we met there was something about you I liked, and trusted."

He traced tiny circles on the upper curve of her breast. "So, I'm kind of like an old shoe, comfortable and pleasant in bed."

Sam twisted again, this time coming to rest against him face-to-face. She trailed one hand down his side. It came to rest on the curve of his hip. "No, Mike. Being with you was far from pleasant. Being with you was... exciting, thrilling." She groped for the right word. "Like fireworks."

His gaze drifted down, then traveled up their entwined bodies to meet hers. "Did I light up your night?"

She laid her hand on his cheek. "Fourth of July."

He shifted and rolled, sliding her beneath him. "How about we let the fuse burn a little longer this time?"

Much later, Mike lay face down beside her, his arm draped over her midsection, his face smooshed into a pillow. Sam gazed at the ceiling. Where did they go from here?

Not once, but twice he'd rocked her world. Was her response something he took for granted?

Or did she rock *his* world, too?

She looked at the bedside clock, surprised to discover it was close to four a.m. As she slid from beneath his arm she cast quick glances at him, hoping to let him sleep. He moaned. Holding her breath, she slipped her pillow beneath his arm. With a muffled grunt, he dragged it close and settled against it. She stood beside the bed, tempted to snatch the pillow away and crawl right back in beside him.

She turned her back on temptation, gathered her sweats and tiptoed from the room, closing the door behind her. In the bathroom she cleaned up and dressed. As she combed her hair, she studied her face in the mirror.

107

It was Christmas Eve, and in the past two days her life had done a sharp one eighty. She didn't look any different, but she'd changed.

A change she couldn't quite put her finger on.

She'd dealt with Al's injury and faced stark danger, and darn it, she'd handled both, and more. She'd struggled a lot throughout her life and figured sheer stubbornness had gotten her through the worst. Somehow she'd managed to land on her feet. Most of the time.

Now, though, she'd been swept *off* her feet.

A fast check found Mike still dead to the world, so she decided to check on her other guy. Darkness still pressed against the windows, but to the east pale, thin light on the horizon peeked through the trees. In dusky predawn feathery snowflakes drifted past the window.

Before she checked on Al, she tossed the clothes she'd laundered yesterday into the dryer. The bloodstains were gone, a big relief, and Mike's jacket had dried on the hanger.

Tomorrow was Christmas, and as she entered the barn she couldn't stop humming a familiar holiday tune. Now it would stick in her head all day. Al's ungainly head rested on the top rail of the stall. He grunted his rough cough-like call when Sam approached.

"G'morning, big guy. I'll bet you're hungry."

She rubbed his soft nose and checked his food and water supply. There was still water, but not a scrap of dried fruit or veggies. After stoking the wood burner, she chopped a Christmas Eve breakfast for Al. His intense dark gaze tracked her every move.

The area she used was designed for efficiency, Grandpa's trademark. Without taking away from the rustic walls, the rustic *feel,* he'd created an efficient, well-organized workspace. Sturdy shelves above and neat uncluttered drawers below. Last night thoughts of Grandpa had taken a back seat. She loved her grandfather with all her heart, and as she worked in his space, chopping thick carrots into pieces, he filled her thoughts and she shook her head, frowning as she scraped carrots aside and grabbed some apples. Guilt drove her troubling train of thought. It was unfair to blame Mike, but she admitted her grandfather hadn't been in her thoughts last night.

She delivered the gourmet moose breakfast of dried fruit and vegetables. As Al lowered his head and began to eat, she laid her head on crossed arms resting on the stall's top rail. Emotions churned inside her. The past two days she'd dealt with anger and fear, but last night's mind-blowing pleasure complicated things.

She lifted her head at the sound of the door behind her opening. Her heart skipped like a stone across a still pond when Mike smiled and crossed to her. His hands came to rest on her shoulders and his fingers tightened in a gentle squeeze. He rested his cheek against her hair.

She leaned against him. "I fixed Al an early breakfast."

"Hmm, lucky moose. How about us?"

"Since its Christmas Eve maybe we'll have cookies for breakfast."

His quiet laugh ruffled her hair. She rested her head against his shoulder. "Mike. I feel strange."

"I think you feel pretty good."

She looked into his eyes. "That was a bit smug. I don't know what to say about... us. I don't know if I'm flattered, embarrassed or pissed off."

His arms came around her. "First, be flattered. I mean what I say, and I say you're a beautiful, sensuous woman. If you're embarrassed, I could surmise it's because you were expecting pleasant, but things went from pleasant to Fourth of July. You're not sure how that happened."

He turned her to face him, touched his lips to hers. "Responding to a lover is nothing to be embarrassed about, and if your response embarrassed you then it's something we need to... explore. I don't know how being with me would piss you off, though, and have to ask, why?"

Sam pressed the heels of her hands to her eyes. "Guilt."

"Why the hell do you feel guilty about what happened between us?"

She dropped her hands, shook her head. "I'm sorry. That didn't come out right. Now you're pissed off."

He linked his hands low on her back and leaned away. His raised brow and tight-lipped smile made heat creep up her neck.

"No, more puzzled than pissed. Why should you feel guilty? Did you rob a bank to buy people Christmas gifts? If you did, I'll expect a new truck when we get out of here."

"No, I didn't rob a bank." She heaved a deep sigh. "You've done it again. Somehow you turn things around. You make me laugh, which relaxes me, and you make me believe everything's going to be all right. How do you do that?"

"It's a gift. I use it sparingly." He loosened his hold on her and tapped her cheek with one hand. "Is Al set for now?"

She glanced at the moose as he munched his Christmas Eve apples. "I'd say he's good for a while."

Mike took her hand. "Then let's get some breakfast and get the day started. I need a full stomach to unravel your phobias."

Chapter Eighteen

Hand in hand they entered the cabin. Sam pulled away and hurried to the window. "Oh, Mike, look, isn't it beautiful?"

He came to her side. The sun was a hazy ball peeking through the falling snow. He draped his arm around her shoulders. Despite the fury of the storm, dawn revealed peaceful beauty.

"Look, over there." Sam pointed as several deer waded through the deep snow following the barely visible roadway. "Aren't they gorgeous?"

"Hmm, they're beauties." Mike leaned closer to the window, squinting at the rolling, white landscape. "The snow is coming straight down now and the wind has shifted. They'll be a gradual decrease in accumulation, but I'd bet the farm this storm set records. I can barely see the top of my truck and yours is totally buried."

"If the snow stops, it will be a perfect Christmas Eve. By tomorrow they could have the roads open. We can dig out." She did a little dance in place, grinning.

"Maybe, we'll see." Damn, he didn't want to dash her hopes, but he knew thruways and side roads would be plowed first. A driveway to a remote cabin was way down on the list. Even if someone made it to the cabin, the news they brought might not be what Sam wanted to hear.

Circumstances may have changed after they'd gotten that brief message from his dad. Doc Gates could be home safe, or he could be fighting for his life.

He placed a finger under Sam's chin, lifted. "Are we going to stand here all day staring out the window, or can a man get some pancakes? In my house on Christmas eve morning, pancakes are a tradition."

She smiled, stretched up for a kiss. "We can't mess with tradition."

He tried to keep things light, meandering into the kitchen as she whipped up pancake batter. "Did you measure all that stuff?"

The whisk whipped hard and fast. "Don't need to. Got it all right up here." She paused, tapping the side of her head. "There's another Christmas eve tradition I'll keep later today. I'll have to dig up a recipe, though. Grandma usually makes it, so this will be my first time."

She placed a cast iron griddle on the stove to heat, gathered utensils and got out plates. She hummed as she returned from the pantry with a jug of maple syrup. She plopped it on the counter and flipped on the CD player. "Later we'll watch A Christmas Story. Another tradition. What does your family do?"

He leaned against the counter, arms crossed, watching her pour batter onto the grill, inhaling the sweet aroma as it sizzled. "We play that same video most of the day. Every once in a while we stop to watch one scene or another."

"What's your favorite?"

"I like the one where Ralph beats the crap out of Scott Farkus."

She flipped the pancake. "Of course you do. You're such a guy."

He shrugged. "Which one do you like?"

"Hands down, it's the one where Ralphie's parents sit by the tree on Christmas night. The holiday's almost over, but there's so much... love. She simply sits beside him in the glow of the tree lights with snow falling outside the window. He wraps his arm around her. They don't have to say a thing."

Her eyes lifted to the window across the room where thick flakes continued to fall. Mike studied her face. Wide blue eyes, skin like cream sprinkled with cinnamon. Untapped feelings swirled inside him. He wasn't sure love was that simple.

Despite his misgivings, Sam's upbeat mood was contagious and the morning flew past. They consumed way too many syrup soaked pancakes, laughing and sharing tales of their Christmas traditions.

"Let's go sit by the fire," he suggested, after they'd cleaned sticky plates and put things away. "I'm stuffed, and I need to take a break."

The fire snapped and danced as they sat side-by-side, shoulders touching. Sam propped sock clad feet on the table in front of the sofa and heaved a deep sigh. He'd fixed a second cup of coffee and, gazing into the fire between sips, asked, "Are you interested in my thoughts?"

She glanced at him. "Thoughts?"

"About your phobias."

"Oh, that. Sometimes I blurt out things and don't know why."

He set aside his coffee and took her hand. "Sam, we're both dealing with a lot right now. It appears we'll spend a major holiday alone together in a remote cabin. Alone being the key word here. When two adults, one male, one female, who know, like and admire one another are tossed into our situation..."

She kept her eyes on the fire, but he detected a hint of smile.

"When two adults like and admire one another," he repeated, "sometimes one thing leads to another."

She turned to him.

He lifted his hand and cupped her chin. "There is no shame, no guilt in anything that's happened between us." He shook his head when she started to speak. "Not done yet. You're worried about your grandfather, and last night your focus shifted. There's no reason to feel guilt or shame in that, Sam. You've doctored an injured moose, baked awesome cookies, kept us fed and trimmed a Christmas tree. You've dealt with it all. I admire the hell out of that kind of strength."

"You make it all sound so noble. You forgot something, though."

"And what was that?"

She squeezed his hand, slanted a coy smile at him. "*I* seduced you."

He settled deeper into the sofa, pulling her firmly against him. "You did. And Sam, the last thing on my mind when we tumbled into bed was wondering if you would measure up."

Using one finger, he tapped her nose. "And don't tell me you weren't wondering just that."

"Maybe, at first," she admitted.

"Sam, my greatest fear was I wouldn't take time and satisfy you. Something snapped when you gave me the green light. I don't understand what it is, but you do something to me."

"So, it wasn't just me who felt like I was about to tumble off a cliff?"

"Tumbling off that cliff doesn't mean you're inexperienced, and because you tumble there's no reason to be embarrassed. You knocked me off my feet. Being with you is damn special."

"Then it wasn't inexperience that made me fall off that cliff?"

"You didn't lose control, Sam, you responded. Control shouldn't be part of making love. Responding is natural. You responded. Correction, *we* responded, to one another."

For a long moment, she regarded him with clear blue eyes. His pulse quickened when she leaned closer.

He pulled her in and kissed her.

Clothes were unbuttoned, slipped off, tossed aside, and the fire warmed emerging bare skin.

He pressed her into the sofa's soft cushions. Flames at his back cast a glow to her skin and reflected in her eyes. She touched his cheek, a familiar gesture now, and that gentle touch set his heart racing.

*****

Sam awoke amidst a tangle of arms and legs. She lay wedged against the back of the sofa facing Mike. Her arms were caught between them, his were around her. One of her knees rested between Mike's thighs. Any higher and well... hmmm.

Slow and even his chest rose and fell against her, a soothing rhythm. She drifted, eyes half open basking in the warmth generated from his body. Her gaze shifted, and her eyes widened.

"Mike." She wriggled one hand free and gave his shoulder a push.

"Humph."

She pushed again, putting more effort into it this time. "Wake up, sleepy head."

He burrowed into her, tucking his face into the curve of her neck. "What is it?" he mumbled.

Slow and deliberate she raised her knee.

He jerked back, eyes open wide now. "Whoa. Could you move your knee? Please," he added, sliding his hand down between them.

"Wake up, then," she repeated. "Look, the sun's up. It's still snowing, but it's bright and sunny."

She scrambled over him. Gathering strewn clothes, she pulled them on as she raced to the window. Sun beamed through it creating a warm, sunny patch on the floor.

"Hurry, Mike. This is so weird. It's still snowing, but the sun is bright." She placed a hand on the glass. "It's warm. You're so slow," she admonished as she dashed past him. "I'm going to get dressed and go outside. There's a snow blower in the garage. I'll bet it's fueled and ready. We can start clearing a path for tomorrow."

"We?" he mumbled, tugging on his jeans. "Got a damn mouse in your pocket?"

She stopped and spun around, grinning. "I heard that, grumpy. You can stay in here. *I'll* run the snow blower."

Mike stood and raked a hand through his hair. Hands on her hips, she tilted her head, watching him. His face was scruffy and fine lines framed his green eyes. He pulled on rumpled clothes.

Two days ago his crooked grin made her remember a little boy. Now that grin, a bit cockier, made her tingle from head to toe.

With a giant yawn, he stretched. "Okay, okay, give me a minute. You're like one of Santa's elves on speed."

Laughing, she went to get dressed for outdoors.

By the time Mike joined her she had the snow blower humming and had shoveled the entryway to the garage. "I'm letting it warm up for you," she called out over the chugging motor. "The top layer is powdery, but down underneath it's packed and hard."

He cleared a path to his truck. She joined him when he shut the blower down and stood examining the impressive hump in the snow. He brushed snow away and blew out a long, hard breath.

She touched his arm. "Are you feeling all right? I keep forgetting about your concussion."

"I feel fine. Not even a headache." Grinning, he pulled off one glove and brushed snowflakes from her face. "You've got snow on your nose."

She wrinkled her nose and tilted her face skyward. "These flakes are so big. I can feel them landing on my face."

His hand cupped her chin and he brought his lips to hers. She closed her eyes, savoring the kiss.

He pulled away and, inches apart, she gazed into his eyes.

"Sam, I..." His gaze skimmed her face. It locked with hers and something flickered in the green depths. She held her breath, waiting, but he never finished. He just kissed her again, this time a gentle touch, not the heat and demand of moments before. He ended the kiss and pointed skyward. "The sun's reached its peak. It'll head down soon and

113

once it sinks low enough it'll be much colder. I won't be able to dig my truck out before that happens. Let's do what we can for now."

Sam glanced at the portion of truck he'd uncovered. Her gaze traveled to another mountain of snow in the tree line. No way could they even get to her Pilot. She could see her breath when she exhaled, long and slow. "You're right."

He stepped away and primed the snow blower. "You go ahead. I'll widen this path and if the snow lets up we can do more tomorrow."

She wanted to know what he'd been about to say before he'd kissed her, but it appeared he'd switched gears and changed his mind. She frowned at his back as the blower roared to life and then trudged back to the garage. Clouds had moved in, swallowing the sun and she shivered as she slid open the garage door.

After Mike guided the machine into the garage, she took a moment to look around at the winter wonderland. She crossed her arms, hugging her body.

Christmas Eve.

Eager to get on with long established routine, she closed the garage door, locked up and followed Mike inside.

Baking Grandma's Christmas Orange Cake was one tradition she'd always carried out under the watchful eye of her grandmother. She'd never tackled the task alone, but she had the recipe and couldn't wait to get started.

She showered. It hovered near freezing outside, but shoveling snow worked up a sweat. Mike offered to take care of Al and disappeared into the barn as she began to gather ingredients for the cake.

He didn't bring up the need to clean out the moose's stall, but she had a feeling he would do just that, which meant he'd have to dump the dirty straw out back.

In the pantry gathering ingredients, she paused staring down at the bag of unbleached flour in her hand. She should have checked the wolf when they were outside earlier. She'd thought about it, but couldn't bear the thought of seeing the unfortunate animal's lifeless, ravaged body. Mike hadn't mentioned it. Not a big surprise. She knew him well enough now to realize he'd let her decide when she was ready to return to the heart wrenching scene behind the barn.

She set up grandma's counter top grinder, gathered one large orange, raisins, and walnuts. She squeezed the juice from the orange, saved it and then cut the orange, skin and all, into wedges.

Mike came in as she dumped the orange, raisins, and nuts into the grinder and started to crank the handle. He was in his stocking feet and as he shrugged out of his coat, asked, "Whatcha making?"

"Christmas Eve Orange Cake. Where are your boots?"

"I cleaned Al's stall, which left my boots kind of funky."

She paused, adjusting the bowl placed to catch the orange mixture.

"You went out behind the barn didn't you?"

He moved to the sink and washed his hands. He finished, cranked off the water, and tore off a paper towel. "It had to be done, Sam."

"And?" she prompted and began to turn the grinder handle again.

"And, I uncovered the wolf and took a closer look." He came to stand beside her, placing one hand one her shoulder. "It was rough, and I hated looking at him, but I knew you'd want to know."

Scraping the bowl, she gave the ground up mixture a stir. "I thought about it earlier." Her voice hitched and she shook her head. "I'm not ready to see him yet."

He gave her shoulder a gentle squeeze. "I figured that out. Better I did it. He had deep gouges in his side, not a pretty sight. If I were to take a guess, I'd say he was desperate and tried to take on a big buck. Mating season for deer is September through December and some of the big guys get downright nasty."

"I suspected as such. Without a pack, taking down a full-grown buck is dangerous, almost impossible to do, too. Plus, if the wolf was ill or weak from lack of food it would play into the mix."

She set the bowl aside and measured flour into a sifter placed over a second bowl. Mike crossed to the fridge and pulled out a beer. "We'll probably never know for sure."

"Get me a couple of eggs and the milk while you're in there," she said and with quick efficient moves snapped beaters into a well-used mixer. "Thanks," she said when he placed two eggs and a half gallon of milk on the counter. She measured shortening and milk into the mixer's large bowl. It hummed to life and, using a spatula, she helped blend the milk and shortening before adding the eggs.

Mike leaned in, watching as she measured more dry ingredients and sifted them together. "I think I know what you're making."

"I doubt it. My grandmother keeps this recipe under lock and key. She'll only give it to close friends and..."

She glanced up and their gazes locked. She broke into a smile. "Your mom, of course she'd share it with your mom."

"It's full of oranges, raisins, and nuts and has some kind of cinnamony orangey topping."

Sam shut down the mixer and scraped the creamy mixture from the sides of the bowl. She folded in the flour mixture and then the orange nut mixture. "Does your mom make it for Christmas? Stop that," she yelped, batting his hand when he scooped a finger through the batter.

He laughed, evading her and sticking the finger into his mouth. "She does. It smells *soooo* great while it's baking, and never made it untouched until Christmas dinner. So, eating it on Christmas Eve became a tradition."

"It's the topping," Sam said as she spread the batter into a large rectangular pan. "I saved the juice from the orange and drizzle it over the warm cake as soon as it comes from the oven. Then I finish off with a mixture of sugar, cinnamon and chopped nuts."

The oven timer dinged and she slid the cake in and reset the time.

As she cleaned up the kitchen, Mike moved to the window, staring out he shoved his hands into his pockets.

Sam finished wiping the counter then went to him. She slid her arms around him and rested her head on his broad back. "You're thinking about them, aren't you?"

"It's hard not to, especially when our traditions keep bumping into one another." He twisted and pulled her to his side, wrapping one arm around her. "Do you believe in fate, Sam?"

The snow outside the window drifted down and waning sunlight streamed through the falling flakes. She rested her head on his shoulder. "Fate or coincidence, somehow we've come to this point in our lives. A truck carrying a moose wrecked and set it all in motion. Where it goes from here is anybody's guess."

Chapter Nineteen

Mike checked on Al as darkness fell and Sam put finishing touches on the Christmas Eve orange cake. The barn didn't seem so stark and chilly now. Wind no longer pounded the windows and doors. The wood burner gave the space a cozy atmosphere.

The aroma of warm cinnamon and orange enveloped him when he returned to the cabin, flooding his head with memories just as warm and comforting. He missed his family. Yet, being here with Sam on this special night took the edge off.

He glanced over as she knelt by a bookcase stuffed with all manner of reading material. No, it more than took the edge off. Being with her stirred feelings and melded them with the magic of Christmas Eve. Two days ago, dropped into a situation he had little control over, he'd been angry and frustrated.

How could things have changed so fast?"

Sam shoved to her feet with a large tattered book clutched in her hands. She turned, a huge smile on her face, and her gaze zeroed in on him. "You're back. I was about to come and get you but wanted to find this first." She raised the book, and then slowly lowered it. "What? Is something wrong?"

Mike shook his head, clearing his mind. "No, nothing's wrong. Why do you think somethings wrong?"

"You look lost in thought, so serious." Her shoulders slumped and she heaved a sigh. "I keep forgetting you're away from home tonight. At least I'm in a familiar place and--"

Two long strides brought him to her side. "No, Sam. Don't go there. I *was* lost in thought, but nothing sad or depressing." He took the book from her hands and laid it aside. Intense blue eyes gazed into his, and he gently framed her face between his hands. "No matter what happens, our time together this Christmas Eve will always be special for me."

He touched his lips to hers. She trembled when he lifted his head and gazed down at her. "I have no clue what the future holds, but I'll never, never," he repeated, "regret the past few days with you."

She bit down on her quivering lip and blinked away moisture gathering in her eyes. "Me neither, Mike."

"So, when do we get to cut into that cake?" He winked and she laughed, blinking away any sign of tears.

Exactly the reaction he wanted.

More than once since they'd been together he'd stood on the edge of a precipice fraught with unfamiliar feelings. Ones he didn't quite know how to handle, which was a first for him.

If he stepped off that precarious edge he could end up looking like a damn fool. He had no experience in this area. No defense against the helpless, light-headed protective emotions Samantha aroused in him, with aroused being the questionable state of being. Love, lust, or whatever, something churned inside his head, inside his body.

Inside his heart.

Sam patted his cheek. "You're in luck. Dessert on Christmas Eve is Grandma's orange cake." She slipped around him and left him staring at the cheerful tree lights. He swallowed the response that had sprung to his lips when he'd thought she'd said 'love' instead of luck.

"Hey," she called from across the room, "I put a ham in the oven when the cake came out, and I have a great way to fix sweet potato fries to go with it."

He swung around, worked up a smile. "And coleslaw, right?"

Laughing, she swiped away silky strands of her dark mahogany hair. At some point she'd freed it, and light caught highlights in the rich glossy waves framing her face.

"You've got that look again. More deep thoughts?" she accused, placing her hands on her hips. When he didn't reply, she shook her head. "I'll make coleslaw, but it's nothing fancy. It's plain and simple with a dressing--"

"You got from your grandmother." He finished the sentence and they both laughed. "I'm going to go clean up. Is there anything you need before I go?"

"No, I can handle things from here. While you were in the barn I showered and all I have to do is change clothes."

As Mike waited for the water to heat for his shower he squinted at his face in the mirror. Whisker stubble rasped under his hand when he rubbed his cheek. A shave, clean clothes and he'd be set for a damn near perfect evening. Did Sam notice how in tune they were with one another? He'd always thought it funny when one of his parents started a sentence and the other finished it.

Moments ago he'd done the same darned thing with Sam, but somehow he did *not* find it funny.

He found it scary.

*****

Sam doused the thick sweet potato fries with melted butter, tossed them with seasonings and spread them on a baking sheet. When the ham came out of the oven she'd put the fries in and make the dipping sauce for them. Everything was coming together.

She glanced out the window and, wiping her hands on the towel tucked into her waistband, moved closer and studied the encroaching darkness. The sky was deep blue, almost black, and snow no longer fell. Off to the north a single star winked against the dark velvet curtain.

His scent surrounded her before she heard him approach, and she sighed when his arms came around her. "Wishing on a star?"

He'd nailed it, but she kept her wish to herself. "Maybe. You smell good." She glanced around. "Nice sweater. You look good in red. Snazzy gray slacks, too. My, my, I'd better go change."

"Another tradition, this one is Mom's rule," said Mike. "On Christmas Eve we can be as casual as we want until it's time to sit at her table. Same goes for Christmas morning. Slump around in PJ's or sweats all morning during the unwrapping madness, but when you come to her holiday table you'd best be dressed for the occasion."

Sam took his hands and stepped back. The slacks were casual and draped well on his lanky frame, and he looked incredibly handsome in the deep red sweater of soft cotton. He'd shaved, and she couldn't resist skimming her hand over one smooth cheek. "The ham is done. I'll go change, and once the fries are done we can eat."

"It smells heavenly in here. I'll try and be strong and wait for you."

She leaned in and nuzzled his neck. Heavenly didn't come close to clean-shaven man, and she gave his neck a teasing nip before she went to change.

A blue and cream scarf and earrings with tiny pearls dangling on thin gold chains dressed up her plain blue sweater. Leg hugging rust colored slacks tucked into low cut soft suede boots completed the outfit. She'd lathered on vanilla scented lotion before dressing. Fair was fair, and if he was going to drive her to distraction with a sexy aftershave she wasn't going to hold back.

When she strolled into the room the look on his face assured her she'd hit the mark.

She just wasn't sure what hitting the mark meant. More than once she'd caught him looking at her in a way that made her feel like a helpless mouse being contemplated by a cat. A big *male* cat.

Whatever lay behind the gleam in those grass green eyes was a mystery. It wasn't her imagination that more than once he'd been about to say something but stopped before whatever he'd been thinking crossed his lips.

She walked to him and he smiled. That crooked, endearing smile that set her body tingling. "Hi, gorgeous." He lifted two glasses filled with sparkling white wine. "I thought we'd start the evening with a holiday toast."

She took the glass he offered and touched it to his. "You read my mind. To our holiday together."

A long moment passed as they sipped, eyeing one another in silence. He'd dimmed the lights until only the tree lights, fat candles on the mantel and on the table glowed softly.

The ham and simple coleslaw were perfect, and Mike insisted the mayonnaise and Sriracha sauce dip she'd concocted for the fries was the best he'd ever tasted.

He raved about the orange cake, touching her more than she was willing to admit. His compliments -- from how she looked to how she cooked -- shouldn't carry so much weight. But they did.

Drowsy and full, they settled on the sofa before the fire. Soft music played in the background. Mike flipped through the pages of the well-worn book she'd handed him before sitting down.

"*Twas The Night Before Christmas*. This is an old copy of a classic." He pointed to the picture of Santa's sleigh on the cover. "I like the old fashioned look. Today they've updated some versions and they're not quite the same."

Sam leaned in for a closer look. "Really? I guess I've never paid attention to any newer versions."

Mike flipped through until he found a publisher name. "I'm going to look for a copy of this one. It will make a nice gift for a baby born around Christmas."

"As your friend Al's baby will be."

Mike nodded silently, staring down at the book.

"Would you do something for me?" Sam placed her hand on his.

He tilted his head, looking directly into her eyes. "Anything I can."

She flipped the pages to the beginning of the story. "Read it aloud."

"Another tradition?"

Sam nodded.

*****

Mike's throat tightened as he picked up the book. He swallowed, stalling to get a grip on the rush of emotion threatening to make it impossible for him to form coherent sentences. It had been a long time since he'd read a story aloud. He'd done a presentation once at an elementary school for the Wildlife Service and had read a story about a mischievous raccoon. The name of the book escaped him, but reading to a group of wide-eyed first graders was a hell of a lot different than reading to a sexy, sweet smelling woman snuggled against him.

Plus, he knew damn well it was her grandfather who'd read the timeless story from this very book.

Big friggin' shoes to fill.

"Mike?"

"I'm good, just getting in character."

She stared at him, humor in her eyes. "You don't have to act out each part."

He chuckled, and the lump in his throat eased. "Okay, here we go.

Twas the night before Christmas and all through the house not a creature was stirring not even a... "

Sam poked his side. "Keep going."

"Moose."

Her laughter was contagious. "Oh, Michael. You've made this day so perfect." She took a deep breath, quelling the laughter, and let it out slow. "Thank you," she murmured and, framing his face between her soft hands, she kissed him.

The book fell from limp hands, and he shifted, deepening the kiss and pinning her against the back of the sofa. Her arms came around him and she gripped his shoulders, her fingers digging in hard.

He broke the kiss and his lips brushed hers as he whispered, "Can the story wait?"

"What story?" she asked, and pulled him in for another kiss.

All of a sudden she straightened and, placing both hands on his chest, gave a gentle shove. "We can't..."

"Oh yes we can," he argued and moved to pull her back.

When she kept him at arm's length, he frowned. "Let me finish," she said, chuckling. "We can't mess up our good clothes. We'll need them tomorrow for Christmas and there're all we've got."

Mike rolled his eyes. "You've got to be kidding."

Sam's gaze pinned him, one brow arched.

"Okay, okay, we'll do it your way," he said and stood to pull his sweater over his head.

His heart skipped every third beat as he stripped off his good clothes, down to his skivvies, while keeping his gaze locked on Sam. "You're torturing me on purpose, aren't you?"

"I have no idea what you're talking about," she replied, her expression deadpan, her movements slow as a tempting stripper as she removed her good clothes and folded them neatly.

Finally she straightened, wearing only her bra and panties. The fire flickered behind her, a perfect backdrop for a tempting silhouette.

"Race you," she said, and shot past him and down the hall.

"Hey, no fair." He tossed his slacks aside and followed.

He still wore one sock and slipped when he careened through the door into the darkened bedroom.

"I'm waiting," she murmured from the bed, her voice an inviting soft purr.

The pace slowed as remaining barriers were peeled away between soft kisses and murmured promises.

Her body was now familiar, yet his need for her deepened as he revisited every curve, every soft secret place that was pure Samantha.

He stroked, she sighed.

Her hands glided up his back and each silken finger left a burning trail that stole his breath away. "Go slow, Mike. I'll treasure this night, and I want to remember every single minute."

His lips trailed over the path taken by his fingers, from the silky skin beneath her chin to the curve of her breast. She lifted, offering, sighing when he took.

In tangled sheets they touched and kissed and teased until their breath came sharp and quick, pushing the pace they'd struggled to contain harder and faster.

Her rapid pulse quivered beneath his lips when he touched them to the soft skin behind her ear. He rose above her and, resting on his arms, he framed her face with his hands and gazed into her eyes.

She took him in, and her eyes closed. He buried his face in the fragrant curve of her neck and they moved as one. Her urgent cries sent him over the edge and pleasure shattered his world.

Mike dozed and Sam's warm body pressed against him. With one leg draped over his, her head rested on his shoulder and each breath she took blew soft and sweet across his bare chest. Stars winked in the midnight blue sky visible through the window across the room.

Technically it was already Christmas. Numbers on the tiny bedside clock read two a.m., yet deep sleep eluded him as he lay wondering what daylight would bring.

Like her wonderful sense of humor, her optimism was contagious. Her confidence that everything would fall into place and Christmas would bring an end to their worry and isolation was unshakable. Throughout the day she'd plowed forward, shoveling snow, baking, carrying out old traditions as if her efforts would make everything come together.

Mike wasn't so sure.

Smoothing strands of dark hair from her face, he smiled when she wrinkled her nose, lifted her hand and rubbed the spot his fingers had brushed. Then she snuggled tighter against his side.

She possessed unbending faith and he'd been caught up in her enthusiasm and simple joy as Christmas Eve drew to a close. She'd welcomed every minute of that day and looked forward to tomorrow, Christmas Day, with the anticipation of a child.

Only it wasn't a child that had stunned him with her impromptu strip before the fireplace. It wasn't a child who'd waited on soft sheets in nothing but sexy as hell underwear.

It was a woman he'd come to admire and respect and... dare he admit it, to love?

The clock's glowing hands crept toward three a.m. Time to shut down and get some much needed sleep. Tomorrow was Christmas. He wished with all his heart that morning brought Sam a wonderful surprise, as was the Christmas tradition.

His heart wished for that, but his mind was more skeptical. He gathered her close and pulled the covers up. Regardless, he'd be there for her, and they'd face the day together.

Hell, who knew? Maybe Santa *would* bring a miracle.

Chapter Twenty

Sam's eyes popped open at dawn. The sky was just beginning to lighten and excitement bubbled inside her as if she were still a child and couldn't wait to see what Santa had brought.

Mike was tucked in against her back. Her butt pressed against him and he'd hooked one arm around her waist, as if to keep her from leaving him while they slept. His chest rose and fell against her back, and his warm breath tickled her ear.

She angled her head to see the time. It was later than she'd thought and she began the process of untangling herself from her bedmate as if easing away from a sleeping lion. Replacing her body with a pillow seemed to work, and she stifled a laugh when he grunted and pulled the pillow tight against him.

She slipped on a pair of cords and pulled on a sweatshirt, minus underwear, and tiptoed from the room. Hunting up anything else risked waking Mike and for whatever reason, she wanted to greet the day and savor the sunrise alone.

Selfish? Maybe, but it was something Grandpa had always done. By the time her grandmother and she had awakened on Christmas morning there was coffee brewing and hot cinnamon rolls waiting.

She heaved a sigh, a little catch in her breath. Grandpa wasn't here this year. Not yet.

When she stepped into the shower the coffee was perked and the rolls she'd taken from the freezer yesterday were ready to pop into the oven. Mike hadn't stirred when she'd tiptoed into the bedroom to gather fresh underwear. Only the tousled top of his head was visible and he'd hardly changed position since she'd left him a while ago. She'd gathered up the clothes he'd discarded in haste the night before, and after neatly folding them, placed them on the bed beside the sleeping man.

As she pulled on the sweater and slacks she'd wantonly discarded last night, her cheeks warmed. Who knew what the future held?

If there even *was* a future for her with Mike.

Last night had been more than coming together physically.

Much more.

Was it possible a link formed all those years ago when they'd been children sparked a reconnection after so long? Or would life take them down different roads and their time together would become nothing more than a cherished memory?

A little sad at *that* prospect, she placed the rolls on a cookie sheet and gathered things to make sweet, creamy frosting to drizzle over them after they came from the oven.

The sound of a door closing followed by the hiss of the shower echoed down the hall. Time to quit pondering what if's, put the cinnamon rolls in the oven and get on with the day.

*****

Hands braced on the shower wall, Mike waited for the pounding water to bring him fully awake. Once he'd finally dropped off in the early morning hours he'd slept like the dead. And he'd awakened alone to discover last night's hastily discarded clothes neatly folded next to him on the bed.

He shook his head, rubbed his hands over his face and lathered up. A short time later he stared into the bathroom mirror while wiping the remnants of shave cream from his face. Part of him wanted time to stand still. That wasn't about to happen, so, what next?

Ever since he'd tracked that damn moose in a blizzard and found a childhood memory in the form of a sexy, grown up woman he'd been attracted to that woman like a moth to a flame.

Tired analogy, but at the moment he couldn't think of another.

Sam had faced a lot, and she'd weathered it all, which was a big part of his attraction. Of course there was her lean, curvy body and eyes so blue a man just wanted to dive in. The danger there lay in the threat of drowning after he dived.

She was frosting rolls that smelled of hot cinnamon and sugar when he walked into the room. In the corner, the Christmas tree lights twinkled. Sam threw a fast glance over her shoulder, smiled and said, "Morning, sleepy head, and Merry Christmas."

He approached her. "Merry Christmas to you, too," he said, and placed a kiss on her cheek. He peered over her shoulder. "How soon can we eat those?"

Laughing, she snatched the bowl out of reach when he attempted to score a finger full of frosting. Her cheerful mood spilled over. How she'd react if the day didn't go the way she anticipated remained to be seen.

"I'd like to check on Al first." She scraped the bowl and, with a tiny smirk, handed the loaded spoon to him. "You're such a little boy."

He took the spoon, licked it clean and handed it back to her. Her gaze lifted and locked with his when his hand brushed hers. After a long moment her eyes softened. She grinned. "If you keep looking at me like that our moose won't get breakfast and we'll be eating stone cold rolls."

"Uh huh," he said, wrapping his hand around hers and rubbed his thumb against her skin. "I'm not a little boy any more, Sam. Grown men like to do a lot more than lick leftover frosting."

"Uh huh. Big girls, too, but..." She sidestepped, gathered up the bowl and spoon and scooted away. As she rinsed them she grinned at him over her shoulder. "We have all day, Mike and it's going to be perfect. Just look outside, it's beautiful. Even Mother Nature helped."

He admired her confidence. As sure as she'd once believed in Santa, her hopes for a perfect ending to this day never faltered.

However, he feared at some point reality would kick in, and when it did he'd be there for her.

Sam donned a lab coat to protect her clothes while she prepared breakfast for Al. The moose paced. His limp was almost gone and there was no blood visible on the fresh bandage Sam had applied the day before. He dived right into his Christmas breakfast of dried apples and wrinkled carrots. If his appetite was any indication, he'd grow into a big healthy moose.

Mike closed the door behind her as she retreated from the stall. "How is the supply of moose food holding up?"

"We're good for now, but his appetite is growing. Grandma won't be happy, though, I'm depleting her cache of dried fruit and veggies." She shrugged out of the lab coat. "Let's go eat. I'm starved."

Upon entering the cabin she paused, listening, gazing out the window. Mike clenched his teeth, reluctant to point out the obvious. Sooner or later she'd be forced to admit nobody was going to magically appear. How to broach the subject weighed on Mike's mind, but he just wasn't sure how, or *when,* to begin.

She poured hot coffee for him and tea for herself while he placed cinnamon rolls on holiday plates. "These plates have been in my family for generations," she said, adding festive napkins beside the plates.

He took a bite of a sticky roll and chewed. Damn, they were good. He hated to ruin such a perfect day, but avoiding the inevitable might make things worse.

"Well, how are they?" Sam asked between bites.

He swallowed and blotted his lips. It was now or never. "Great, they're great. Ah, Sam, I think we need to--"

"Shhh." She held up her hand and jerked ramrod straight.

"What's wrong? Are you--"

"Quiet," she snapped, and shoved to her feet. "Don't you hear that?"

Frowning, Mike pushed back from the table and, heaving a sigh, followed Sam as she dashed to the window.

Late morning sun slanted through the trees and untouched snow shimmered as if covered with sparkly diamonds. A male cardinal, bright red against the winter backdrop, flitted from branch to branch. Nothing else moved in the morning stillness.

He placed his hands on Sam's shoulders as she leaned in, listening and peering out at the winter wonderland. "Sam, I think it's time to face the truth and ..."

The cardinal took flight and the distinct buzz of an engine filled the air seconds before the first snowmobile crested the hill. It paused, engine revving, then swept down the slope toward the cabin.

With a loud whoop, Sam dashed for the door.

"Sam, wait! Son-of-a-bitch," he muttered, grabbing their jackets as he followed her. The door to the cabin banged open and nearly smacked him in the face as he trailed behind her. When he caught up with her he shoved her jacket at her. "Thanks," she said, shrugging it on and glancing sideways at him." Sorry about the door."

Beside him, she bounced on the balls of her feet. God help them if whoever barreled down that hill toward them brought bad news. He slipped on his jacket and wrapped his arm around Sam's waist. She quivered as they waited, leaning into him when he pulled her tight against him.

Seconds before the snowmobile swung around and stopped in front of them a second, then a third whining machine crested the hill and swooped toward them. Bundled in winter gear and wearing helmets it was impossible to identify the riders. There were two on the first one, a single driver on the second, and two on the last one.

Sam broke free and rushed forward the minute the first engine cut out. The driver removed his helmet and pulled off a dark ski mask.

With a smile as wide as the sky and blue eyes, as bright and clear as his granddaughter's, Charley Gates dismounted, opened his arms and laughed aloud when Sam rushed into them.

Charley's passenger lifted a hand and smiled at Mike. "Merry Christmas, Michael," she called out.

"The same to you, Mrs. Gates," he replied, and muttered to himself, "It sure is now."

The other two snowmobiles pulled up and shut down. To Mike's surprise, Herb and Lillian Brown rode the last one, and his chest tightened when Al, his best pal and co-worker, crawled off the second machine.

Al bypassed the hug fest going on with the other arrivals and strolled toward Mike. "Looks like you still haven't learned how to drive in snow," he said, angling his head toward Mike's truck, barely visible in the drifted snow behind them. "And did you ever find the damn moose?" He pulled off one thick black glove and stuck out his hand.

Mike took hold, and for a long moment they just stared at one another. Then Mike shook his head and, placing both hands on Al's shoulders muttered, "Son-of-a-bitch. I sure am glad to see your ugly face. And yes I found the damn moose."

Eyes wide with surprised, Al scoffed, "You're kidding, right?"

Mike laughed. "He's in that barn behind me eating his breakfast."

Lillian Brown herded them toward the door. "I don't know about the rest of you, but I'm freezing and my butt's sore. Herb, grab that chest

127

and let's get inside and get this party goin'."

"Did you clean out Brown's General to fill that chest?" Mike teased, and helped Herb unstrap the big cooler.

"Why not, it's Christmas," Lil replied. She paused, touching Mike's arm and aiming a warm smile at Ellen and Charley Gates, who still had Samantha wrapped tight in their arms. "I think it's one we'll all remember for a long time."

As they filed into the cabin, Mike held Al back. "I'll fill you in about the moose once things calm down, but first, and more importantly, how is everything with you?"

"Everything is perfect. I've got a son, Mike. Your sister, my beautiful wife, gave me a son and they're waiting for me."

"Shit," Mike muttered, then huffed out a short, sharp breath. "Congratulations, my friend. You've been in my thoughts."

Al slapped his hand on Mike's back. "Same goes, Uncle Mike. Let's go inside and get caught up with things. I promised I'd be home in time for Christmas dinner and my butt is in the wringer if I'm not."

Mike followed, grinning. "Hey, where's my cigar?"

Chapter Twenty-One

Everyone talked at once, and Samantha embraced every second of the swirling confusion. Her eyes filled when Lil handed her a bag of Peppermint Patties in a festive bag. "Figured you'd be ready for a sugar hit," said Lil. "There's not a single one left in Brown's General. Stop that." Using her thumb, she wiped a tear from Sam's cheek. "You gave us a scare, young lady." She titled her head toward the group of men across the room. "Remind me to thank Mike for tracking you down," she said and wrapped her arm around Sam's waist, pulling her close.

Sam slid her arm around Lil in return and leaned into her. Since they'd burst into the cabin she'd been swept up in the excitement and pure joy of the moment. Her grandmother was busy unloading the chest the men had dragged in and Lil's Herb was helping her grandfather cart in more firewood.

Her gaze swept the room until she spotted Mike deep in conversation with Al. His head turned and green eyes, bright with laughter, zeroed in on her and held.

Lil patted her arm. "I'm going to go help Ellen get all the food we brought unloaded." Her sharp gaze bounced from Sam to Mike. "Hmm, Mike looks awful darned happy about something."

When Lil moved away, Charley Gates eased in beside Sam, slipping his arm around her waist. She pulled her attention from Mike and smiled up at her grandfather.

"So," Charley remarked, rubbing his chin. "Looks like you and Mike have had quite an adventure."

Her heart faltered and her cheeks heated. "Ah, I guess we have."

He gazed down at her, then at Mike, then back to Sam. "Lil said he lit out after you as soon as he knew you'd headed out in the middle of a blizzard." His tone and steady gaze made her feel like a ten year old. Only she wasn't ten anymore, and her grandfather was well aware she'd just spent several days, and *nights,* with Mike Donovan.

She cleared her throat and swallowed. "Maybe heading out alone wasn't such a good idea, Grandpa," she said, "and if I'd known you'd been taken to the hospital I'd have come to be with Grandma."

He blew out a short, harsh breath. "Indigestion," he grumbled. "I told your grandmother it was nothing more than that, but she wouldn't listen and hauled me to the ER. I'm healthy as a darned horse, and plan to be around for a good long time." He tightened his arm around her and she rested her head on his broad shoulder. He smelled of Old Spice and spearmint gum, as he had for as long as she could remember.

"Now, tell me about this moose you patched up? I only got bits and pieces with all the yammering when we first got here. Sounds like you did okay, though."

"I think he'll be all right, Grandpa. He's in the barn."

"Then let's go have a look at him."

*****

Mike sipped coffee as he filled Al in about the past few days. His friend listened wide eyed as he described the moose rescue and the wolf encounter. "She patched up a five hundred pound moose as if she'd been doing it all her life, and damn it, Al, my knees were shaking when we faced off with that wolf. Sam is one smart, brave woman."

He hesitated, not sure if he wanted to reveal the more personal aspect of his feelings about Sam.

As Sam and her grandfather left the room, Al eyed Mike over the rim of his cup. "Besides being brave and smart, Samantha Gates is a damn good lookin' woman. Being marooned here alone with her for two or three days must have been... interesting," he concluded, eyes twinkling with humor.

Mike shrugged. "We survived."

Al shook his head. "You survived? Bullshit, I've known you way too long. The way you two look at one another it's a wonder sparks don't fly. I'd say you did a lot more than survive."

"Okay, we did more than survive. A hell of a lot more," he added and glanced over as the door to the barn closed behind Charley and Sam. "If you've noticed the chemistry between Sam and me, Charley Gates has too. Maybe that's why he keeps looking at me as if he's considering hauling us into town with a shot gun at my back."

Al's laugh got a few puzzled glances. He slapped Mike on the back. "Charley may be protective, but he's also realistic. I won't pry, but I knew damn well when I crested that hill and saw you with your arm wrapped around Sam your life had changed."

"Changed?" Mike muttered. "More like a monumental shift."

"Trust me, you'll live." Al glanced at his watch. "If I help, are you up to pulling your truck out? Along with everything else, I heard you took a nasty blow to that rock hard head of yours."

Mike grimaced, rubbing his forehead. "It's still tender, but symptoms of a concussion have disappeared. After Sam took care of the moose she patched me up and then insisted on, ah, spending the night real close to keep an eye on my condition."

Al's brow lifted. "Uh huh, I'll bet you resisted that idea." He winked. "You can tell me the rest over a cold beer once life gets back to normal." He finished his coffee and glanced around the room. "Looks like everything's under control here, let's go dig out your truck."

130

Sun warmed their faces as they made their way up the slope to Mike's truck. "Sam named that big ugly moose Al, by the way."

"No shit?" Al brushed snow from the truck's hood. "Well, I guess I'm honored. He'll be a famous moose once this story hits the papers. Every animal rescue group in town was ready to help find that injured moose until the blizzard shut things down. They'll be thrilled. You two will be heroes."

"I'd just as soon let our moose continue on his interrupted journey as soon as we can arrange for it without attracting a lot of attention. Once I'm back to work we can arrange to transport him to Adirondack Rehab. They'll have to decide where Al goes from there."

*****

After Sam's grandfather examined Al's leg, he replaced the bandage and stood. He brushed straw from his trousers. "That's a heck of a job, honey. Well done," he said and gave Sam's shoulder a pat and a rub.

She stepped away from Al, pleased her moose had behaved himself. When they'd first entered the stall he'd shied away and moved to the far side of the enclosure. She'd talked softly, stroked his neck to settle him and, other than a few wary sidesteps, her grandfather's exam went well.

They exited the stall and stood side by side observing the moose. "I acted on instinct, Grandpa. If I'd stopped to think about the whole situation I might not have been able to function."

"You're a natural, Samantha. I've known that since you were a little girl." He turned to face her. "Now I want to hear about the wolf."

She knew when she'd told him what had happened he'd want to see the wolf for himself. Everything had been too fresh, too recent for her to look at the wolf's body any sooner. Her grandfather wouldn't force her, but his presence gave her courage and now the time had come for her to revisit the site where she'd faced life threatening danger and almost lost.

As they trudged through the snow, she relayed how everything had played out that night. "In hindsight, it wasn't very smart to come out here alone, but we hadn't heard the wolf for a while and I based my decision on that," she explained, glancing back at her grandfather.

"Best to think about how smart doing something is *before* you do it young lady. Being decisive is fine, but this was a valuable lesson. Learn from it," he added.

She stopped just short of the fallen wolf. Her grandfather touched his hand to her back then stepped around her and knelt down. Carefully, he brushed snow from the wolf and leaned in, shaking his head. "He was in bad shape, honey," he said, threading his gloved hand through the wolf's sparse coat. He leaned closer, running practiced hands over the lifeless body. "Look at these deep gouges in his side, and I can feel at

131

least one broken rib, there's probably more."

"Mike suggested maybe he tried to take down a buck by himself."

Her grandfather nodded. "I wouldn't be surprised. On his own without a pack this poor guy's chance for surviving were slim to none, especially when the storm hit."

Sam dropped to her knees beside him. The paralyzing rush of emotion she'd feared dissolved, replaced by overwhelming sadness. "I wish I could have helped him, Grandpa."

He rose and pulled her to her feet. "Sometimes there's nothing we can do, Sam. This appeared to be one of them." He wrapped one arm around her. "You said Mike was angry at first when he'd found you."

"I think angry is putting it mildly. It was stupid of me coming out here alone, and I put him at risk when he had to come looking for me."

"I'd have to agree with Mike, but I give him credit for taking care of you throughout this whole ordeal." He nudged her toward the barn. "We'll have to wait a while to give your wolf a decent burial. It could be spring before the snow melts and the ground thaws. As soon as possible I'll do an exam and we'll see if we can piece together what happened to this poor guy. In the meantime, you can fill me in on what you did between sparring with a wolf and doctoring an injured moose."

They closed and locked the door behind them. She'd known eventually they'd get around to discussing Mike. Both grandparents were well aware she'd been isolated with Mike for several days. She knew them well. Without saying one word, Grandma's knowing smile and Grandpa's grave expression spoke volumes.

Before they returned to the cabin they checked once more on Al. She rested her elbows on the top rail of the stall. "I don't know if I'd have been able to do what I did without Mike," she began. "It was scary at times, but without him..."

"Mike Donovan is a fine young man. His parents were relieved when they got that cell phone call. It was brief, but at least they knew you were both safe."

She turned to him. "I was so worried about you, Grandpa. Mike risked his life for me to get that phone and call his dad. After that call I knew you were alive. It helped me deal with the rest."

Her grandfather heaved a sigh. "Your grandmother--"

"Loves you," Sam declared. "As I do, and I don't blame her one bit for making sure you'd be here for both of us for a very long time."

He pulled her in and hugged her. "Let's go see what's going on inside. I know Lil and Herb are staying, but I think Al wants to get back to his new family." He eased back and met her gaze. "Mike will want to head home, too. I imagine they'll have a devil of a time uncovering his truck. If they can't, he can always ride back with Al. We trucked all three snowmobiles as far as the turn off from the main road on trailers. The roads are..."

Mike will want to head home.

Sam's good mood nose-dived. She hadn't thought about Mike leaving so soon.

"...in decent shape, but we knew the only way we'd make it back here was with snowmobiles and when the snow let up we--"

"Grandpa, I have to find Mike. I have to say goodbye."

His gaze lingered on her face and he nodded slowly. "Then let's get back inside and make sure that happens."

Herb was sprawled by a roaring fire and Lil was checking something in the oven. Her grandmother was at the sink filling a teapot.

Sam cast frantic glances around the room. She spotted Mike's duffle by the door and demanded, "Where's Mike?"

Her grandmother paused, and her brows snapped together. She shifted her gaze to Sam's grandfather.

"I'm going to go clean up," said Charley. He tilted his head toward Sam and lowered his voice. "Talk to her," he said, and disappeared down the hallway.

Sam's grandmother turned to her. "What is it, honey? Is something wrong with the moose?"

Sam sucked in a deep breath. She reached for her grandmother's hand. "No, he's fine. Grandpa says he's fine."

"Then what's wrong? You're white as a sheet and your hands are like ice. Don't tell me everything's fine."

"Where's Mike, Grandma?"

"Sit," Ellen insisted, gesturing to the table. "Mike's with Al digging out his truck." She squeezed Sam's hand and gestured to the table. "Sit. Digging out that truck will take a while. I'll make tea, it'll warm you up and you can tell me what's got you so upset."

Sam stirred sweetener and cream into her tea. She'd been so excited when everyone first arrived. There'd been so much going on. She'd been busy with Grandpa. Mike had been busy with Al. Of course she'd known Mike would want to go home and be with his family, eventually. Time had slipped away, and now Mike was leaving. She wanted to tell him how much he meant to her, and if he left without saying goodbye... well, damn it, she'd never forgive him.

"So, what's on your mind, honey?" Her grandmother sat across from her. Grandma had always been there for her, and she thanked God she was there now to help her unravel feelings churning in her head.

In her heart.

"I don't know where to start, Grandma." She rubbed between her eyes and frowned at her steaming tea. "Do you believe in love at first sight? I mean... can love happen, like, all of a sudden?"

Her grandmother reached across the table and took one of her hands. "Aww, I think I understand why you're so rattled all of a sudden, and yes, my dear, I *do* believe in love at first sight."

Sam looked up. "You do?"

Fine lines deepened around Ellen Gates' eyes when she smiled. "Honey, I met your grandfather on a blind date, a Friday night movie followed by burgers and fries at the local hangout. By the time I went to work Monday morning I knew I was in love."

"Just like that?"

"Just like that, except you've got to remember that was many years ago." She tucked in her chin and arched one brow. "I knew I loved Charley, but things didn't move quite as fast as I suspect they do today."

Sam bit her lip and heat crept up her neck. "Warp speed, Grandma."

Her grandmother chuckled. "Samantha, I'm going to be blunt. If you're holding back, questioning your feelings, or Mike's," she added, lifting that one brow again, "then the only way you're going to find out is to lay your cards on the table. Then depending on the outcome, you'll either plan a future together or move on alone. It's that simple."

Sam tightened her grip on her grandmother's hand. "I've fallen in love with Mike, Grandma. I've never felt like this before, but I don't have a clue how he feels about me."

"You don't, huh? Let me ask you this. I'll not pry into what happened here between you two, but I have my suspicions. If I'm right, I don't think Mike is the type of man to walk away and not look back."

Sam glanced at the duffle by the door. "I didn't either, but it appears I could be wrong. How do I find out?"

"You tell him how you feel about him. If he doesn't return your feelings and *then* walks away, well, you're better off without him."

Gazing across the table, Sam held tight to her grandmother's hand. Minutes passed and a million scenarios filled her head.

The door to the cabin swung open and Al walked in. "We got the truck out and finally got her started. Mike's afraid she'll cut out so he sent me for his stuff."

Sam jumped to her feet. "Wait, Al. I'll take him his duffle."

Al grinned. "I thought you might want to do that."

She turned and held up her hand, fingers crossed. Her grandmother winked, leaned forward and whispered, "My money's on Mike."

The door to Mike's truck stood open and he waited in the opening, leaning on the truck's roof, arms crossed. He straightened when Sam appeared in the door and, shoving his hands into his pockets, stepped away from the truck and waited.

"Everything all right in there?" he asked as she approached.

Without answering she stopped in front of him and dumped the duffle at his feet. "All day yesterday I had a feeling everything was going to be all right."

Frowning, Mike shifted his feet and nodded. "Yes, you did." He shrugged. "I didn't," he added. "I fried my brain trying to figure out how

I'd deal with things when today came if nobody showed up. Worse yet, I feared somebody *would* come and bring bad news."

"Well, sorry about frying your brain with my optimism, but right now I'm not too optimistic. Damn it, Mike. Were you going to leave without saying goodbye?"

He stuffed his hands into his pockets and poked at snow with the toe of his boot. "I'm not good at feelings, Sam, or long goodbyes."

"I'm in love with you, Michael Donovan." She huffed a breath. "Now you know. Go ahead and leave if you must. I'll just have to deal with it."

Strained minutes ticked by, but when his shocked expression slid into his familiar, crooked grin, the messy stew of anger, fear, and disappointment churning inside her went soft and warm.

"You just lifted a ten ton weight off my shoulders. Hell, Samantha, I love you too." He opened his arms and she rushed into them. "I've been driving myself nuts trying to figure out what all the stuff going on inside me meant. Was it the situation, the isolation, or maybe just plain lust?"

She leaned back, frowned up at him. "I wondered about the lust factor, and when I thought you were just going to walk away without saying goodbye I was so mad at you."

He grinned down at her. "Maybe there was a little lust."

She poked his side. "Maybe a little," she agreed. "But alone, lust didn't work for me. There was too much more happening. All I know is I couldn't let you leave without telling you how I felt."

He framed her face with his hands and touched his lips to hers. Her heart beat strong and steady, yet emotion bubbled up inside her. When the kiss ended, a happy tear escaped. "I don't know where we go from here, Mike."

He swept his thumb over her cheek and wiped the single tear away. "Hey, we'll work things out. Where we go from here isn't a problem, as long as we end up together."

"Hey!"

Arms around one another, Mike and Sam turned toward the cabin.

Al stood, hands on his hips. "If you let that truck stall I'm not going to help you get it started again." He grinned, waved and went back inside and closed the door.

"I have to go be with my family now," Mike said.

"As it should be, and I'll be with mine."

He kissed her again. "Do I have a date for New Year's Eve?"

"Always, Michael Donovan. This year and for the rest of our lives."

The End

About Nancy Kay

Nancy Kay resides near Lake Erie in Western Pennsylvania with her husband, a former member of the Marines and the Pennsylvania State Police Department, who provides valuable insight for her stories. Nancy is a member of Romance Writers of America and two affiliated chapters. Her stories are set in small towns and inland communities along the shores of the Great Lakes. The stories focus on romance, intertwined with love of hearth, home and family, yet sprinkled with suspense, danger and intrigue.

Learn more about Nancy at www.nancykayauthor.com.

Made in the USA
Columbia, SC
10 November 2017